PEGGY BIRD

author of *Unmasking Love* and *Ringing in Love*

A Holiday for Romance

The *Gift* of Love

CRIMSON
ROMANCE

F+W Media, Inc.

Published by
Crimson Romance
an imprint of F+W Media, Inc.
10151 Carver Road, Suite 200
Blue Ash, OH 45242. U.S.A.
www.crimsonromance.com

ISBN 10: 1-4405-7044-2
ISBN 13: 978-1-4405-7044-5
eISBN 10: 1-4405-7045-0
eISBN 13: 978-1-4405-7045-2

For Maggie, who shared her birthday with Isabella as well as her love of Friday the thirteenth, and Sophie, who not only loaned Isabella her curly hair but also taught me how to take care of it. You are the best granddaughters on the planet!

Chapter One

The last thing Isabella Rodriguez wanted for her birthday was a book on how to find herself. The accompanying condescending remark from her oldest brother Luis about how she was wasting her life and needed to read the book, and the nods of agreement from her three other brothers, made it worse. She wanted to throw them—and their gift—out of the house.

She tried to lower her blood pressure and calm her anger by taking a few cleansing breaths. Unfortunately, what was effective in her yoga class didn't seem to work anyplace else, so she gave up the attempt and let her emotions win. "I don't need anyone's advice on how to live my life, Luis. Especially not yours." She was sure steam was coming out of her ears.

Luis continued as if he hadn't noticed anything—the words, the tone, or the steam. "Look, Izzy, it's not just me. All four of us agree. We love you. But you've been living for free in Dad's house ever since he died while the rest of us cover the taxes and the cost of keeping it maintained. The house was left to all of us, not only to you. Those of us with families would rather support our kids, not our sister. I don't know if we're more frustrated or worried that you seem hell bent on living like some trust fund kid on our mutual inheritance but—"

"My name is Isabella," she interrupted. "Bella, if you must shorten it. Never Izzy, in spite of your continued use of the horrible sounding name. And I'm twenty-seven, not a kid."

"Okay, whatever, *Bella*," Luis said, his hand slicing the air in an impatient gesture. "But your name was all I got wrong. The rest is dead on. You haven't had a serious job since you left California. It's like you just stopped living when you moved to Portland." He ran his fingers through his mop of curls, one of the few traits Bella and all her brothers shared. "God knows we've tried to help. How many contacts did we give you in the real estate business here? Contacts who might have had a job for you."

"I didn't realize pressuring me to take the jobs in the family business no one else wanted was help. Or trying to set me up with a job I didn't want. I thought it was just interference. As this is."

Luis ignored her comment and went on with his lecture. "You shouldn't bear *all* the blame for where you are in life. Mom and Dad indulged you because you were their baby girl. But Mom and Dad are gone. It's time to get over being spoiled by them."

The mention of her parents punched her in the gut. As the only girl, the youngest in the family, and a late in life surprise for her parents, she'd had a special closeness with them both. And taking care of them in the last years of their lives had only strengthened an already strong relationship. Especially with her father, who'd had a particular soft spot for her. The empty space left by his death the year before was a lot smaller now than it had been right after he died, but it was still there. She missed him. Badly. No more so than today, her birthday.

If he'd been alive, this would have been a joyous celebration. He loved throwing parties for his kids, even when they were grown up. When her four brothers had said they'd all be bringing their families up from California for her birthday, Bella had visions of a family reunion and a party close to what her father would have arranged. It was serendipitous her birthday fell on a Friday this year, making it possible for them to all make it to Portland in time for dinner and, she had hoped, a weekend together. Friday the thirteenth of July would be her lucky day, she thought.

Except it hadn't turned out at all as she'd expected. Her celebration, it seemed, had merely provided an excuse to call a meeting to handle a crisis—her. She should have known. The four men never all came to Portland for anything other than a family matter to take care of. A new roof for the house. Papers to be signed for the business. Their father's funeral. She was in the same category as home repairs and memorial services. She hadn't figured it out until her three sisters-in-law took their kids and hightailed it out the door right after eating the dinner she'd carefully prepared for everyone. Leaving their gifts for her to open without them, they made no excuses and didn't say goodbye. They waited until she was in the kitchen after clearing the table and left, abandoning her to the mercy of her brothers.

What a stupid fool she had been to actually think her siblings cared about her birthday. All they cared about was their own agenda.

At least Luis had brought up the subject of her future after the women and children had hit the lifeboats for the safety of the shore. Or wherever they were headed. The *one* good thing about all of this was that he'd had the courtesy not to embarrass her in front of her nieces and nephews.

Luis glanced over at her second oldest brother Ernesto, a signal to run with the conversational ball, apparently. Great. They were tag-teaming her. She wondered if they'd scripted in advance what they were saying.

"It's time we stop paying for you to have a carefree life, Izzy," Ernesto said. "Most of us have families, kids to support. We want to sell the house so we can finally get our part of the estate."

"Still Isabella. Still not Izzy."

"Jesus, Izzy, is that all you get out of this conversation? We use a nickname you've never liked?" Carlos, the next brother in the lineup, chimed in.

"What I'm getting from this conversation is that you four, as usual, are making decisions that affect me without any consideration of what I might want."

Luis looked like he was about to interrupt and bring the conversation back his way, but she wasn't going to let him. "You had your say, brother. Now it's my turn." She raised her eyes to meet his gaze so directly she swore he flinched. Good. Maybe he finally saw how angry she was.

"I have done everything this family has ever asked of me. When I graduated from college, I went into the family real estate office like I was expected—no, *ordered*—to do. I didn't complain. Instead, I worked my way up from receptionist to running the place. But you couldn't let me enjoy my success for long, could you? I was told to move to Portland to take care of Mom and Dad. I didn't object even though I had friends and a life in California." Her hands fisted with the anger she still felt from having it all yanked out from under her when, two years before, her mother had been diagnosed with cancer and her aging father had been unable to manage her care. Because she was the only girl, she was expected to take care of her parents. So she met her obligation like the good daughter she was.

From the sideways glances Luis and Carlos exchanged, she knew she'd hit a nerve. "I'm an equal part of this family, and I don't deserve to be talked to like this." She turned to Javier, the brother closest to her in age and affection, who was sitting beside her on the couch. He looked uncomfortable, like he wasn't happy with how the conversation was going. "Javier, how could you do this to me on my birthday?"

"I'm sorry, Bella," Javier said. "We probably should have picked another time. But we've been talking about it for weeks, and since we're all here ..." He let his words trail off and shrugged. "We thought it would be better to tell you in person, and who knows when we'll all be together again." He tried to put his arm around her shoulders, but she scooted over to avoid the hug.

"We need to get this taken care of," Luis went on. "The real estate market's recovered; houses are selling; it's time. Besides, don't you want something better for yourself? From what I can see, all you do is rattle around in a big house, writing short stories you can't get published while you study off and on for a real estate broker's license."

Before she could respond, Javier added, "A broker's license I don't think you ever really cared about getting." Over her weak attempt to ward him off, he took her hand and squeezed it. "I'm right, aren't I? You really don't want to get into the real estate business, do you?"

As much as she resented having to admit one of the brothers was right about anything, Javier was correct. She had only said she'd study for the test because she thought the family wanted her to. It had never been her idea to become a real estate broker.

"Look, whatever-your-name-is," Luis said, "you did a great job running the office in California, and we all agree you were amazing taking care of Mom and Dad. I don't know what we'd have done without you. But that was then. This is now. We need to close out the estate. And the truth is, the fat bank account Dad left you when he died is getting low. You don't have to go back to the family business if you don't want to. But you do have to find something you want to do that makes you enough money to support yourself in a place of your own. That's reality. You can't afford to keep this house going, and we don't want to do it anymore."

"If Dad were still alive, you wouldn't dare do this to me." She knew she was tearing up, but she was determined not to cry in front of them.

"If Dad were still alive, we wouldn't have to do this. But he's not. And we do. End of story." Standing in front of her, Luis tried to pull her up from the couch. "Don't be angry, Isabella. We're only trying to do what's best for all of us." He, too, reached to put an arm around her. "Give me a hug to show me you understand."

She refused his hand and his hug, standing without his help. Drawing up to the full extent of her five foot two inch height, she glared at him and stuck out her chin. "What I understand is this is a hell of a way to wish me happy birthday." She picked up several empty coffee cups from the cocktail table in front of her. "All right. If you all agree it's time to sell the house, I guess I'm outvoted. Put the house on the market. If that's what you came for, you have it. Now I think it's time you all left. Until it's sold, this is still my home. So I have the right to have whom I want here, especially on my birthday. And right now, that doesn't include any of you. Go back to your families and your expensive houses and luxury cars and leave me alone." She was tired of the discussion, tired of trying to fight the inevitable. She only wanted them to be gone so she could mourn the end of yet another phase of her life brought on by the demands of her family.

Luis shrugged and, after trying one more time to kiss her goodbye, headed for the door accompanied by Carlos. Ernesto patted her on the arm before he joined them. Javier stayed behind, looking even more uncomfortable than he had before. "I'm sorry. I wish there were ..." he began but didn't seem to know how to finish. Instead, he changed the subject. "How about I stay and help clean up?"

"No, it's okay. I can do it myself. And don't worry about the others. I've been steamrolled by those three more times than you've had hot meals. I'm used to it."

She turned so he wouldn't see the tears beginning to fall and escaped to the kitchen. In a few minutes, she heard the click of the deadlock indicating Javier had left and locked up after himself.

Two hours later, Bella had run a couple loads in the dishwasher, bundled up the tablecloth and napkins for the laundry, and swept up the cookie crumbs her nieces and nephews seemed to have deposited in every room on the first floor. Pouring herself the last of the wine from dinner, she settled in the living room again, surrounded by her father's books, art glass, and the plants she struggled to keep alive only because he'd loved them so much. She tried not to replay the conversation she'd had with her brothers, but it was hard not to.

The worst part was she knew in her heart, no matter how mean it was of them to spring it on her at her birthday dinner, they were correct—it *was* time to sell the house. She might not want to join the family business, but she knew enough about it to understand they needed to take advantage of the improved real estate market.

Which meant she had to do what she'd been avoiding ever since her father had died—figure out what was next for her.

Luis accused her of having no focus. That wasn't true. She'd always had focus. Granted, it hadn't been on her own dreams and ambitions. Instead she'd concentrated on what her family wanted her to do. Ever since she'd been a kid, she'd tried to be the perfect daughter. She listened to her parents. Didn't cause any trouble. Didn't object when the rules for her brothers were different from the rules for her. Gritted her teeth when her father—and often the oldest of her brothers—cross-examined her friends like a prosecutor in a high-profile criminal case. She knew how much her father adored her. Knew he was going to those extremes to do what he thought would protect her. She never complained. At least, not to him. She understood that her father and, later, her brothers were overprotective because she was the baby of the family, a status she seemed doomed never to outgrow.

And, no, she hadn't pursued her interests. She'd listened to her parents when they said her writing would never pay the bills. Instead, she got the business degree the family wanted from the college the family insisted she attend so she could work in the home office of the family real estate business. Like the family wanted.

True, in return for doing what her parents asked her to do, she'd been protected her whole life. Her father had cosigned for her car loan. Her mother slipped her extra money every now and then. And when she moved to Portland, they completely supported her in exchange for her taking care of them.

When her father died, she lost more than her last parent. She lost her moorings, the sense of security they'd given her. It had upset her so much that she'd done a couple foolish things in the months following his death. She'd spent more money than she should have on new clothes, for one. Worse, in a desperate attempt to keep from having to worry about any of the messy details of carving out a life of her own, she'd tried to latch on to a family friend in the hope he would marry her. Thank God Marius Hernandez had been in love with someone else, which saved her from the terrible mistake of marrying someone she didn't love solely for the security of being taken care of.

After her aborted plan to seduce Marius into marrying her blew up in a very public and embarrassing scene at the Portland Art Museum in front of half the art lovers in the city—and the woman Marius loved—she'd almost been frozen in place, unable to decide how to head her life in a direction that would make her happy. In the past year, she'd only made two decisions of any note. First, she decided to stay in Oregon out of her brothers' reach so they wouldn't be able to "help" her anymore. The scene after her birthday dinner showed how well *that* decision had worked out.

The second decision had been more successful, however. She'd gotten a part-time job, which she loved, with an interesting company run by a woman named Summer Olsen. Maybe that was a place to start. She could ask Summer to help her with her decision. A decision that would be based on what she wanted, not on what her family expected. This time, she'd make a plan for her life based on her goals and ambitions. As soon as she figured out what they were.

Somewhere, under the layers of the "good daughter" who'd been there for years, was a woman who had dreams and desires, just like everyone else. All she had to do was drill down deep enough to find her. And she'd better do it fast. The house wouldn't take long to sell.

•••

To fast-track the beginning of her new life, Bella turned to her boss, the owner of "Break Up or Make Up"—or as everyone called it, BU/MU (pronounced Boo-Moo). The firm offered counseling, group sessions, legal advice, and practical assistance to people who were trying to fix broken relationships, either personal or professional. The founder, Summer Olsen, and Darcy Ross, a combination office manager and writer, were the only full-time staff. But the roster of consulting psychologists, social workers trained in counseling, and lawyers, all of whom worked with clients on a contract basis, was extensive. There were also writers available to ghost letters from clients to about-to-be-ex business partners or lovers when clients couldn't or didn't want to do it on their own. Bella had been one of those writers for almost two years, gradually moving from a few hours a month to what was now a half-time job. In spite of what her brother assumed, it paid rather nicely.

Bella and Summer had scheduled lunch the Monday after Bella's family dinner to celebrate her birthday. It was the perfect opportunity for her to pick her boss's brain about ideas for what she could do or people she should talk to who could help her figure things out. Summer knew everyone in Portland worth knowing and would be only too happy to help, Bella was sure.

When she arrived at the BU/MU office, the very pregnant Darcy greeted her with a birthday card and a hug made awkward by her belly before waving Bella into the boss's office.

"Happy birthday, sunshine," Summer said, barely glancing up from her computer. "Give me a few minutes to finish up what I'm doing here, and I'll be ready to take you out for a birthday lunch." When she looked up to get a response, she frowned and looked over the tops of her red-framed reading glasses. "Sorry. I guess I should say, happy birthday, raincloud. What's up?"

So much for putting on a good face.

Bella shook her head, then nodded before shaking her head again.

"Good to see you're clear about what the problem is. Want to talk about it?"

"I planned to wait until lunch to talk to you, but maybe it would be better to get it off my chest now. Mind if I take the victim's chair?" Bella dropped into the seat in front of Summer's desk where her clients usually sat.

"You know I don't like to call my clients victims. Well, not most of them. What's going on?"

"My brothers announced at my birthday party on Friday they're selling my house—my dad's—*our* dad's—house. And they told me I'm a spoiled brat who needs to grow up and find herself."

"Ouch. Happy birthday from your loving family."

"Yeah, well, the truth is, however angry they made me by bringing it up on my birthday, they're sort of right. I haven't really gotten things together in the year since my dad died. I've let it slide because I could. And now I'm not sure how to start. I haven't really had a lot of practice setting goals for myself. In the past, my goals have been dictated by what my family wanted."

"I thought you wanted to write."

"Okay, let me be more specific: I haven't figured out what I want to do to make enough money to support myself. Writing fiction sure hasn't done that and won't for the foreseeable future. The payments for the dozen or so pieces I've had published barely cover the cost of gas for my car for a month. And even if I finish editing one of the novels I have drafted and get lucky enough to find a publisher, I'm not well known enough to make much money at it." She waved a hand helplessly in frustration.

"I'm sorry you had such a rotten birthday dinner. What do you need to cheer you up?"

"Actually, I need more than cheering up; I need advice. I was going to ask you if you could help."

Summer had been sitting back in her chair with a funny look on her face. Now she took her glasses off and leaned forward on her elbows, staring across the desk for a few moments before saying, "Actually I might be able to give you more than advice."

Still lost in the memory of her disastrous birthday party, Bella didn't pick up on Summer's subtle change of subject at first. "If you have some ideas about a career counselor or someone else I could talk to, please, feel free to give me some recommendations. I'm totally at sea about what to do next. But whatever it is, I have to do it soon because I'm pretty sure the house will move quickly in the current market."

"I'd be happy to recommend a counselor if you still want one after I tell you about my idea." Summer picked up a yellow legal pad, then flipped it back onto her desk. "I've spent the last couple days trying to write a job description for an ad to find someone to manage this place while Darcy is on her six-month maternity leave. She's due at the end of September, and I need to find someone soon so I can get her—or him—trained before she leaves. But the more I tried to describe who I was looking for, the more I became convinced I was going about it the wrong way. You could be the answer to my problem."

"If you need help writing the job description or the ad, I'd be glad to draft it for you. Just tell me what you're looking for."

"I'm not suggesting you write the copy; I'm suggesting you take the job."

Too stunned to answer for a few moments, Bella searched her friend's face expecting to see a "gotcha" look or a smirk. Instead, Summer's face seemed to say she meant it. "Why would you want to hire me?"

"Playing down your abilities is not exactly how you get a job, girlfriend." Summer tore several sheets of paper off the pad and crumpled them up. "If I'd thought of this days ago, I could have saved myself the struggle of trying to describe what I was looking for. All along, I've been looking for you."

"Me? How do I qualify for the job?"

"Well, I want someone with experience managing an office—and from the way you've described your family's real estate business in California, you were in charge of an operation a lot bigger than this one. Next, I want someone who's a good writer—which you've certainly shown you are." She lobbed the paper wad into the recycling basket. "And I want someone who knows what we do and is enthusiastic about doing it. Again, you fit the description."

"Are you sure?"

"Absolutely. Don't you see? We can solve each other's problem. Working for me for six months will give you time to get your feet on the ground and figure out what you want to do next. And hiring you means I won't have to go through the trauma of finding and training someone new for only a short time. Or, even worse, hiring people from a temp service who won't be able to do what I need done. And I won't have to get used to having someone strange in my office every day. I already like having you around. It's a classic win-win."

Bella agreed with much of what Summer had said. She understood and supported what Summer was trying to do with her business. And the two women not only got along but also worked well with each other. They'd met at a City Club of Portland lunch. Bella had been there to connect with someone her brother Luis had wanted her to get to know. Summer had been there to pass out her business cards to people at the lunch table. The guy never showed up, but the two women had clicked.

It was a big leap from part-time writer and friend to full-time office manager, though.

"It's simple: I need you and you need me."

"If I said yes, what would you be willing to pay?" Bella asked.

"Exactly what I pay Darcy: $4,000 a month plus medical and dental. Does that cover what it would cost to rent an apartment and keep your little bit of metal you call a car on the road?"

"I think so. Plus I still have some savings from what my father left me." She closed her eyes as she realized, for the first time since her birthday dinner, she felt hopeful. "Okay. I'm in. Where do I sign?"

"Think about it while we have lunch. We can talk contract when we get back." Summer stood up and grabbed her purse. "Let's blow this popsicle stand. I'm starving."

"All of a sudden, so am I," Bella said.

Maybe, she thought as they walked toward Twenty-First Avenue, this wasn't the worst birthday of her life after all.

Chapter Two

As he strode down Spring Street in downtown Seattle, Taylor Jordan was on a high having nothing to do with artificial stimulants. He'd just done a ninety-minute presentation followed by a Q and A session with the management committee of CloudCo, one of the up and coming high-tech firms in the city. They'd loved his recommendations for a strategic business plan and growth strategy for the company. Loved him. It had been worth every single hour he put into the damn thing to hear them praise his work and insist he continue on with them to implement what he'd recommended. The president of CloudCo had been on the phone raving about him to one of the senior partners of Taylor's firm, MBA Consulting, as he left the conference room. The odds of making partner at MBA had gone from "possibility" to "sure thing" in the course of one meeting.

He'd spent over six months working on the project. Long days. Few weekends off. Eighty hours most weeks for the past couple months. Well, maybe the last three months. His personal life had paid a high price. He hadn't done anything socially for months. Had barely managed to return phone calls, never saw friends.

And he'd neglected—her word, not his—Allison, the woman he'd been dating for the past year, while he slaved away, first on the research and then on the report he'd just presented, while also juggling his other projects and responsibilities. Even though he thought Allison understood he was doing it for them, to ensure their future together, he had a sense she was getting tired of being alone on the weekends, conducting way too much of their relationship by text and e-mail supplemented by the occasional late night phone call and dinner when he could squeeze it in.

However, now that he'd presented his report, he was ready to make up for lost time. He had a surprise for her that he was sure would fix things.

The idea had come to him one night after he'd gone home so wound up from working on the CloudCo project he couldn't sleep. Wired for sound after too much coffee and the adrenaline surge he got from writing the perfect introductory chapter for his report, he'd found himself at his laptop writing out a "to do" list for the weekend he was planning for Allison after he did the final client presentation. As he typed, he got an idea. Why not make it perfectly clear to Allison what he had in mind for them as a couple? And what better way to show her he'd researched all the important things they'd need to consider than to give her a report on his ideas.

He began with a cover letter telling Allison how much he cared for her and how happy he would be to partner with her as her husband. Then he Googled "engagement rings" and uploaded images of rings he could afford—without including the price, of course—and asked her to select the one she liked the best.

Next he researched honeymoon sites and added his pick of what he found to the report, complete with pictures of beaches, restaurants, and tourist activities at each location. For good measure he listed Zillow links for half a dozen houses around the Puget Sound as examples of the home they'd buy when they got back to Seattle. He even had a list of proposed groomsmen and a few open dates for their wedding the following summer.

Thinking it would be fun to make it look like a real consultant's proposal, he had it printed and bound with a bright red cover and their names inside a heart on the front. The guy at the FedEx Office store looked at him a little oddly when he explained what it was but he knew Allison would love it when he presented the finished product to her sometime during their long weekend at the coast. He'd known from the first time he'd met her how perfectly she fit into his plans for his life. All he had to do was show her, with his research and report, the logic of their being together permanently as a married couple.

Ever since high school, Taylor had planned each step of his life with the same care he gave each client report. He was determined not to end up like his father had, making and losing several fortunes with asinine business decisions and harebrained investments. Only too aware his childhood could hardly be called stable, Taylor had done everything within his power to minimize the risks of things going wrong in his adult life.

For example, to ensure he'd get into the right college, he participated only in high school activities that looked good on his college applications or gave him experiences he deemed important to his goals. He researched classes, teachers, and colleges with a thoroughness astounding to his advisor in high school. She gave up trying to give him advice when she discovered all the groundwork he'd already done before he came into her office.

In college he never put a foot wrong. No stupid drunken parties. No bad grades. No careless relationships with inappropriate women. Grad school was the same.

His plan included work for a high-tech firm in some capacity for a short time then a switchover to a management-consulting firm where he would focus on helping high-tech businesses start up, grow, and succeed. No one associated with any business he helped would ever end up the way his father and his family had.

When he left grad school, he had offers from a dozen or more firms in his field of choice. He carefully vetted each one and chose a small company where he worked for two years. Then he signed on with MBA Consulting. It had been the right move. He was challenged by the variety of clients he worked with, able to use his extensive education in business management, and was considered an asset to the company. He would only miss one goal. He set out to be a partner by the age of thirty-five. If he made it this year, as it now looked like he might, he would only be thirty-four.

Part of his plan had been to find a woman sometime in his middle thirties who could appreciate his commitment to his career as well as to his future with her. Of course he hoped they'd care for each other, but love wasn't at the top of the list of things he was looking for. Love hadn't played much part in his parents' relationship. It never could if there was no financial security, in his opinion.

He was sure he'd found everything he wanted in Allison. An engineer with the Bellevue office of a big international firm, she was as much a professional as he was. She worked hard, knew what it took to get ahead. Craig, an old college friend of hers and an acquaintance of his, had introduced them at a business-after-hours cocktail thing, and she'd impressed the hell out of him. They had so much in common it was astonishing—even having attended Stanford at about the same time and on full-ride scholarships, although they'd never run into each other on campus in the year they'd overlapped. Both were Seattle born and bred; both were enthusiastic fans of their hometown and everything in it (although her favorite sports team was the Mariners baseball team and his, the Seahawks football team).

She was smart and ambitious. She dressed professionally for work and attractively when they went to dinner. In heels, she was only a couple inches shorter than his six feet four. And her blond hair and blue eyes, which almost perfectly matched his, would guarantee, genetically, children who would be tall, fair, and good looking.

All the signs were there. This was the relationship he needed for the next stage of his life because Allison Lindberg was, in short, the girl of his—and any other ambitious man's—dreams.

Everything was falling in place. The perfect job and the perfect woman added up to the perfect life. He had it all under his capable control. He'd never have a life like his father's.

Eager to share with Allison the results of his successful meeting at CloudCo, Taylor called her cell as he walked back to his office.

He immediately got voicemail, which he assumed meant she was on another call. But when he tried again after he returned to his office, the same thing happened. Finally he called her office number. The department's administrative coordinator was cool, saying only that Allison was gone for the rest of the day. Which didn't explain why she wasn't answering her cell, but Taylor couldn't get any more out of the adco.

By the time Taylor got back to his office, the news of his success had already made its way from one cubicle to another in his firm. It had even penetrated to the offices on the outer edge of the floor where the big girls and boys played and plotted behind their closed doors while they looked out the windows at the cityscape only they were privileged to see.

The chairman of the firm's partnership committee, Nate Benjamin, led a parade of committee members into Taylor's cubicle. "You won't believe what the CloudCo guys are saying about your work. I don't think I've ever heard so much glowing bullshit from a client." The grin on his face belied the backhanded compliment.

"Thanks, Nate. I was happy with what they said, even if it was B.S."

"You earned your pay this month. Nice work." He stuck out his hand. Taylor stood to shake it, and Nate clapped him on the back with his left hand. He'd been slapped on the back so many times since he'd returned from his meeting, he was sure his suit jacket was wearing thin from the pounding. And as he winced, he wondered if he'd even have a bruise or two in the morning. Which reminded him somewhat painfully of his need to get back to the gym. If a few slaps on the back were bothering him, it was past time to make up for the months of not working out.

"A couple members of the partnership committee and I would like to take you out for a drink after work tonight. You won't even have to use any of the bonus you'll be getting to pay for it. You free to join us?"

Drinks with the partnership committee? Even if he'd had plans, Taylor wouldn't have turned that down. "I'd love to. Thanks."

"Great. I'll stop by about six thirty, and we can go downstairs together."

As soon as Nate left, Taylor made one more attempt to talk to Allison but, when he got voicemail again, left a message asking her to join them at the bar on the ground floor of his office building so she could be part of the celebration, too.

This was turning out to be one of—maybe *the* best day of his life.

• • •

Taylor was a little buzzed. Three Manhattans in an hour and a half on an empty stomach will do that to a guy. Luckily, he used public transportation to get to and from work. But being a responsible transit rider didn't help with opening the two security locks on his apartment door. Somehow the keys didn't seem to be working right tonight. Eventually, he got the right key into the correct lock without putting a dent into either his euphoric mood or the door. He was happy. Very, very happy. Which is also what three Manhattans and the best day of his life will do.

He knew he should get something to eat, but he didn't want to lose the glow so he plopped down in his favorite chair and replayed his personal highlight reel from the day: The look on the faces of the CloudCo management committee when he finished his presentation. The conversation he overheard between his boss and the president of CloudCo as he left the conference room. The kudos from Nate Benjamin when he got back to the office. The drinks and praise from the members of the partnership committee. The congratulations from his girlfriend.

Wait. No, he'd never talked to Allison. She hadn't shown up at the bar to celebrate, either. He should call her again.

The doorbell ringing interrupted his fumbling for his cell. He looked out the peephole and saw a guy in jeans and a sweatshirt with the words "Break Up or Make Up" and two hearts, one whole, one broken in two, splashed across the front. He was holding a large manila envelope.

When he opened the door the man said, "Are you ..." He consulted the envelope, then said, "Teej?"

Allison was the only person who called him Teej. This had to be from her. Maybe this was her way of congratulating him on his success. "Yes," he said, his eyes having a bit of trouble focusing on the man in front of him. "My girlfriend calls me Teej."

"Okay, then, I have a delivery for you." He handed over the envelope he was holding.

"What is it?" Taylor asked.

"Don't know. Only know it's for you. Sign here." The delivery man held out a clipboard, and Taylor scrawled an indecipherable signature at the bottom of the form. "Thanks. Have a good one." The young man disappeared down the hall toward the elevator.

What the hell is this all about? Taylor stood in his doorway looking at the envelope for longer than he should have. In his half-buzzed state, it seemed important he figure it out before he opened it. But he wasn't having any success, so he closed the front door and went back to his living room.

Returning to his favorite chair, he squeezed the envelope. *Hmm. Nothing lumpy or bumpy. So probably not a pipe bomb.* Not that he'd know what a pipe bomb felt like. Besides, if it was for Teej, it had to be from Allison and it wasn't likely she would send a pipe bomb anyway. An exploding device wouldn't be a good way to congratulate him, would it?

He turned the envelope around so he could see the return address. *Portland? Why would she be sending something from Portland? It must not be about my CloudCo success. She wouldn't have had enough time to get something here from Portland in the last couple hours, would she?* Moving the envelope back and forth like a trombone slide, he tried to read the name of the company, which was slightly smeared—probably from the light rain he had noticed when he left the bar. It looked like it said "Break Up or Make Up." *Hmm. That's the name the delivery guy had on his sweatshirt. Weird name for a company. Wonder what they do?*

Finally giving up on figuring it out, he grabbed the gadget he used to slice envelopes and opened it. Inside was a single page letter.

Dear Teej:

I know you're going to be hurt and angry about the contents of this letter and even angrier at how I'm choosing to get the message to you, but I'm desperate. I haven't been able to have a decent conversation with you in months about anything, much less something important. And it's past time for me—for us—to stop pretending everything's going well with our relationship.

Relationship? Who am I kidding? E-mails and texts between people who live two miles away from each other don't make a relationship. A relationship happens when people care about each other enough to make time for each other. For the past six months—for half of the time we've been seeing each other—your job has trumped everything personal. I know how much you want to make partner and why the CloudCo project is important. I have big projects and goals, too, yet I still have room in my life for someone I care for. You don't.

It's been obvious to me for months, we need to break this off. You probably would see it, too, if you were less focused on your work.

I've learned through counseling how important it is for me to get out of this stressful situation—yes, that's what it has become, a stressful situation, not a relationship. Craig recommended this company in Portland. They've helped me work through my issues and craft this letter. They could help you, too, if you'd let them. I've enclosed their business card. Call them.

Please don't contact me. I've gone away for the weekend. I know you and know you'll come banging on the door of my apartment trying to talk me out of this decision. I don't want to be there when you do.

I'm sorry it has to end this way. You're a nice guy, Teej. Someday, maybe, you'll look up from your computer and see what's out there. When you do, maybe you'll find someone you care for and want to let her in. But it won't be me.

Allison

Taylor had never sobered up so fast in his life.

How could she do this? She knew he thought she was the perfect person for him, didn't she? Okay, maybe he'd been a little busy lately, but it didn't mean he didn't care for her. He'd been working for them, for their future.

He didn't know what the hell he was supposed to do with his plans to ask her to marry him, to be his partner, to live in a perfect house like the ones he'd picked out. What would he tell people who asked him where she was? How would he explain how some dumbass company in Portland had helped her dump him? A dumbass company she went to because the same guy who'd introduced them found a way to break them up. What kind of bullshit was that? What kind of crazy place tells people when to dump their boyfriends? What kind of man does that to another guy?

He had wasted time researching houses and honeymoons for *this*? For *her*?

He'd never thought she was this kind of person. Of course he hadn't. Because she *wasn't* that kind of person. At least, she hadn't been until she went to this place, this ... whatever it was ... in Portland. They were to blame. If they hadn't existed, Allison wouldn't have gone there. And she wouldn't have sent him the letter. She'd have spent the upcoming weekend with him, and he'd have smoothed all this out.

"Fake Out/Make Out/Take Out"—whatever the hell they called themselves—had talked her into this. His problem was with them. So, since they created the problem, the solution was for them to fix it. If Allison had believed them about breaking up, maybe they could convince her to come back to him. If he had to, he'd hire them to tell her she made a mistake.

He'd call them. Give them a chance to redeem themselves. No, his still half-fuzzy brain rejected calling as ineffective. Better to go there in person. They should see firsthand what they'd done to him so they could feel remorse for causing him this humiliation. Then they'd have to help. He'd drive to Portland. He'd take his marriage report and show them what a good boyfriend he was. He'd make them see who he really was, and they'd get Allison back for him.

But not tonight. No business, even a whack job one like this, would be open by the time he'd get to Portland. And even if it was, he shouldn't be driving. He'd taken extra days off for the weekend at the beach he was supposed to have with Allison, but since his romantic trip wasn't going to happen now, he'd use the time to drive to Portland and get this straightened out.

Chapter Three

For the first time in years, Taylor slept through his 6:00 a.m. wake-up alarm. When he startled out of sleep at eight, his head was achy, his eyes burned, and he was confused. Why was he sleeping in his suit? Why was he so tired? Why wasn't he at work? Then he remembered. CloudCo. The Manhattans. Allison. The awful letter. His canceled weekend away.

Without showering, shaving, or changing, without doing anything but gulping down a glass of tomato juice and a handful of Tylenol, he ran out of the house and raced to her apartment building, hoping she had lied about being out of town. When pounding on the door got no response, he knocked on her neighbor's door. Through a space only as wide as the door chain would allow, the neighbor confirmed what the letter had said—Allison was gone. She had left her cat Maxine with the neighbor to feed. The neighbor said she didn't know where Allison was. Taylor suspected she was lying. But the door was slammed in his face before he could say anything more.

He had only one move left—he had to get to Portland. He raced from the building, checked to make sure he had enough gas in the tank, pointed his car south, and, at an appropriate and well-within-the-limit speed, headed toward Portland and the people who had wrecked his plans.

. . .

Four hours later, Taylor pulled up at the address on the business card enclosed in Allison's letter, a colorfully painted Victorian in Northwest Portland. It looked innocuous, if a little garish, not how he'd expected a den of vipers would look. There was no sulfurous odor emanating from the place. No ogres guarding the entrance.

Also no parking space nearby. After he'd cruised the neighborhood for a few minutes looking, one opened up a block away from his target. He slipped his Prius into the space and let his righteous indignation propel him up the street to the office of Break Up or Make Up.

Where he was even more disappointed. The house wasn't inhabited by demons after all. Instead, a perfectly normal, even attractive, pregnant woman was seated at a glass-topped desk at the back of the entry hall of the old house. The nameplate in front of her proclaimed her to be Darcy Ross. She looked up with a pleasant smile on her face as he walked in. "Hi. Welcome to Break Up or Make Up. How can I help you?"

Taking a few moments to settle himself so he didn't rip into the woman with his complaints, Taylor looked around. Glancing to the left, he saw what must have originally been the living room of the old house, now converted to a waiting area. The door to what was probably the dining room behind it was closed, as was the door at the end of the entry hall. Steps before the closed door led to who knows what fresh hell upstairs.

All the rooms he could see were painted a pleasant sky blue, the wood floors had been refinished to a high gloss, and the furniture in the waiting room was a series of soft, comfortable looking couches covered in some sort of pale yellow fabric, which looked all sunshiny and cheery. The art on the walls was mostly restful landscapes.

These people even manipulated you with color and visuals to make you calm. Was this operation a front for some sort of cult? Maybe Allison was being led into the jungle to drink Kool-Aid. No, Allison was too smart to fall for something dangerous. Although she'd fallen for their other line of B.S.

"Sir?" the receptionist said. "Can I help you?"

"I'm here to see the owner," he said, returning his attention to the front desk and trying to sound businesslike but firm. Consulting the card Allison had included in her letter, he added, "Summer Olsen. I'm told she owns the business. I want to see her."

"Do you have an appointment?"

"No. But it's important. I drove down from Seattle this morning especially to see her about this." He waved Allison's letter at the receptionist. "To find out what she's going to do about it."

The receptionist lost some of the warmth of her smile. "She was in conference a while ago, and I'm not sure she's finished. But I can slip her a note. Can I tell her who's asking to see her?"

"I don't care what she's doing. I have to talk to her. I told you, it's important. Really important." He could feel the little bit of control he had on his emotions slipping as his voice got louder. Loss of control was an almost unknown and definitely uncomfortable feeling for him.

"I have to talk to her. I have something to show her." He took the red bound marriage report from under his arm and put it on the receptionist's desk. "Something to show her what a mistake she's made. She has to help me."

The receptionist glanced at the report but didn't pick it up. "I'll make sure she knows you said it's important. But I still don't know who to say is here."

"Tell her Teej is here. She'll know who I am." He could feel the last vestiges of control over his temper disappearing as he brandished the letter from Allison at the receptionist again. His voice, which up to this point had been rusty from lack of restful sleep, probably some loud snoring, and a slight hangover, now broke into an almost preadolescent pitch as he said, "Surely she knows the names of the people whose lives she wrecks. Tell her I'm here to straighten out the things she messed up with this letter. I can't leave until she sees me."

The receptionist looked uncertain at best, frightened at worst. "Okay, I'll tell her. But can't you give me more than just Teej?"

"She'll know, believe me." By this time, he was pacing in front of the desk, running his fingers through his already wildly messy hair. "I need to talk to her. There's not much time. I have to get this settled."

The woman rose from her desk. "Why don't you take a seat in the waiting room, and I'll see if Summer is available to see you."

He could tell from the way she spoke she was trying to calm him down. He wanted to say, "Tell her to get her ass out here, lady," but instead he repeated, "It's important I talk with her right now."

The look on her face didn't give him much hope it was going to happen.

• • •

Bella heard the commotion in the outer office but didn't think too much about it. Probably another street person had wandered in, asked for a handout, and didn't like the answer he got. She continued her report to her boss. "So, next week I have ..."

The door to Summer's office in what was once the back parlor of the old house opened, and the receptionist slipped in. "Sorry to barge into your meeting, but there's someone here who's asking to see the owner."

"Is that who's making all the noise out there?" Summer asked as Darcy carefully closed the door behind her.

"Yeah, he's kinda agitated. He looks like he spent the night under a bridge—his suit's rumpled and his shirt's a mess, although both look pretty expensive. He hasn't shaved. His eyes look like he hasn't slept much. And he's pale as milk."

"Did he say why he wants to see me?" Summer asked.

"He keeps saying something about a letter."

"A letter? Uh-oh. Maybe he got a break-up letter. Did he give you a name?"

"Sort of. He said to tell you he's Teej. He wouldn't give me a last name," Darcy said.

"Teej? The name sounds familiar, doesn't it, Bella?"

"Absolutely it does," she said. "Don't you remember? I wrote a letter for a woman in Seattle to someone she called Teej. She wouldn't give me his full name, only his address. She said she didn't want to expose him to any more embarrassment than she already would be by sending him the letter."

"Yes, that's him," Darcy said. "He said he drove down from Seattle. What do you want me to tell him?"

"I think I remember the name." Summer shook her head. "Tell him it's company policy to protect our clients by not seeing people we've delivered letters to. If he has an issue, he should take it up with the person who sent him the letter. If they want help reconciling, I'd be happy to recommend someone for couples counseling in Seattle."

Bella chimed in. "From the tone of the letter she wanted, there's no hope of getting back together. The guy's a workaholic who ignored her for six months while he worked on some project. It didn't make it into the letter, but in one of our conversations, she told me she didn't think he really loved her as a person anyway. More like he loved the idea of her. And she said in the letter she'd be going away so she wouldn't be around when the letter was delivered."

"Remind me who the client was?" Summer asked.

"Allison Lindberg. Nice woman. At least, from our phone conversations about her break-up letter, she seemed like she was."

"Of course. She originally asked only for a letter, but after we talked, she asked for a referral to a counselor so she could figure out why she kept falling for guys who never put her first. She's the woman who insisted on doing her counseling here, instead of Seattle so she didn't run the risk of damaging her about-to-be-ex's reputation. I only met her in person once, when she came down for her initial appointment with me."

Summer rose from her desk. "Would you rather I handle this, Darcy?"

"No, I'm fine. I don't think he's dangerous, just upset. I don't think you'll solve anything by getting into a conversation with him now anyway. He's too wound up. You stay here. But lock the door in case I'm wrong and he decides to hunt you down."

"Okay, but we'll be listening. If it sounds too confrontational, one of us will come out. I don't want you to put yourself in any danger." She nodded toward Darcy's belly. "You can't run too fast carrying the little one around."

Bella followed the receptionist to the door, closing and locking it after her. "While you listen, Summer, I'll pull up the contact information on Allison Lindberg. I think she needs to know "Dear John" has turned into a ranter of the first order. He may be after her next."

● ● ●

"I'm sorry, Mister Teej. Summer can't see you. She's in a meeting but asked me to say ..."

"I knew it. She won't deal with the consequences of her actions. Damn it," he shouted. "I don't care what she's doing. I drove here from Seattle to see her and get this mess," Taylor waved the paper around again, hoping the words would fly off the page and convince the receptionist to do as he asked. "... this mess settled." He pointed to the report on the desk. "This will show her how wrong she was to poison my girlfriend against me, to wreck my plan. I need to get it sorted out." He'd been fuming the whole time he'd been alone, pacing the waiting room, his anger growing with each minute the receptionist was gone. The owner's refusal to see him was gasoline on the coals of his fury.

"Please let me finish. She asked me to tell you it's company policy to protect our clients by not dealing with the recipients of the letters they send. You should talk to the person who asked us to write the letter."

"I'd love to, but you convinced her to leave town and I can't find her." He was sure by now his voice was loud enough to be heard a block away. He couldn't remember ever being this out of control, his voice not only getting louder but also rising to a tone that would hurt the ears of all living creatures that heard it. "You people are irresponsible. You don't care who you hurt, what you do to the lives of others." He started in the direction from which the receptionist had returned.

She moved as fast as she could to try to get in front of him. "I'm sorry. You can't go into the offices. Staff only."

"I'm not going to invade anyone's office. I only want to make sure your owner can hear me." He dodged Darcy's attempt to block him and took two more steps into the hall before raising his voice even louder. "You may ignore me now, Summer Olsen, but I'll make sure you find out who I am. I don't know how. But I *will* make you pay for the terrible thing you did to me."

He grabbed his marriage report from the desk, escaped from the building, and ran down the street. He sat in his car for several long moments, steaming. They shouldn't be able to get away with what they'd done. He had to do something. Maybe if he talked to a couple of their neighbors, he could find out some gossip about them, give him an idea of something he could do to get back at them for what they'd done.

When he had himself under some control, he approached a couple of the houses on the street where the BU/MU office was located. Several people refused to talk to him probably based, he realized later, on his wild, unkempt appearance. The few who would talk to him only said having BU/MU in the neighborhood sometimes caused parking problems. Otherwise, the company was an okay neighbor.

Hardly the information to get him the revenge he was hoping for. He gave up his quest and left Northwest Portland hoping the drive back to Seattle would help him think of a better way to make good on his promise to Summer Olsen.

By the time he was home, he hadn't come up with any legal, much less ethical, ways to get back at Break Up or Make Up. In addition, as he cooled off and his saner self emerged, he realized how dangerous it might be to his chances of making partner if he tried to damage a small business.

But he was also sure he was in the right and resented the feeling of powerlessness to prove to Summer-what's-her-name how wrong she was. However, if there was nothing he was willing to do, he reluctantly decided he'd better let it go and hope karma would sort things out.

He'd pick up the pieces of his plan and get on with his life. He comforted himself with the knowledge that all the rest of the plan was working. He'd even have enough money from the bonus he'd be getting from the CloudCo project to use as a down payment on a new place to live, where he didn't have to pay rent. A condo would be nice.

For the foreseeable future, however, he would definitely not be looking for a new girlfriend. Not until he could be sure the next woman he got involved with was ... well, he wasn't sure what she'd be. All he knew was she wouldn't be anything like Allison. She would understand how she fit into his plans for his life and be happy to be part of it.

Chapter Four

Eight months later

Bella was wrapping up a phone call when Summer came into the BU/MU office and placed a cup of coffee on her desk.

When the call was finished, Summer explained, "I thought you deserved a treat today. I think you like salted caramel mochas, don't you?"

"You are my goddess. I love them!" Bella took a sip of the drink and moaned her appreciation. "This is what heaven tastes like, I'm sure. I hope you got yourself one, too."

"Based on your recommendation, I did. And you're right. It's delicious."

"So, tell me, how come I'm getting this unearned treat?"

"Like hell it's unearned. You've been amazing taking over for Darcy. You mastered everything you needed to learn in only a few days. I didn't have to hover over you at all. I should have brought you a mocha every morning."

"As much as I love them, a daily salted caramel mocha is probably not part of a healthful diet," Bella said. "But as a treat, it's about as good as it gets. Thanks."

Summer started toward her office but stopped halfway down the hall and, without looking back, said, "When you have five minutes, can you come into my office? There's something I want to talk about with you." Without waiting for an answer, she proceeded to her office and closed the door.

Uh-oh. Now what? Bella tried to think if anything had gone wrong in the past few weeks, anything she'd screwed up, but nothing came to mind. Then the obvious occurred to her. They were coming to the end of Darcy's maternity leave. Summer would be telling her when the job was over. That had to be it.

The past eight months had been some of the best in her life. Using the skills she'd developed managing her family's real estate office, she'd quickly taken over the daily operation of the BU/MU office. Summer seemed happy to let her run things her own way, even giving her the latitude to tweak a few of Darcy's procedures. And she gave Bella additional letters to ghost.

When she told her brothers about her "new" job, they had asked a lot of questions, conveniently ignoring the fact she'd been working for Summer for almost two years. When they insisted on investigating BU/MU to make sure it was a "safe place" for her, Bella was furious and asked if they'd entered some contest to see who could be the most overprotective brothers on the planet.

She was embarrassed but felt she had to tell Summer what was going on. Summer had laughed it off. Of course, no red flags showed up, and Luis reluctantly told her they "approved" of her new job.

Surprisingly, the house took a while to sell. There were lots of showings but no offers until a man who planned to retire to Portland bought it. He agreed to a rent-back agreement with Bella until he was ready to move, which, until recently, meant she didn't have to apartment hunt at the same time she was looking for a place to work after Darcy returned to BU/MU.

She'd fallen into a comfortable routine, which her boss was about to remind her would soon change. At least, that's what she assumed the meeting would be about.

Bella procrastinated for fifteen minutes, finishing up her coffee, sorting papers on her desk, and checking the client roster for upcoming due dates before deciding it would be best to get the bad news over with.

She knocked on the door to Summer's office and, when she heard "Come in," entered. Deciding it would be better to rip off the bandage herself she said, "I'm ready for you to tell me when

I need to vacate Darcy's desk. I imagine you called me in here to give me a date, didn't you?"

"Partly but mostly ..." Summer leaned over the desk with a big smile on her face.

"You don't have to beat around the bush," Bella continued. "Part of me hoped she'd like being a new mom so much she'd want to stay home permanently and I'd be able to move into her job, but I knew it wasn't likely to happen."

"It wasn't. But I have another ..."

"You've been terrific to work for. Between the experience I've gotten here and the reference you wrote for me, you've given me what I need to find a similar job. The letter of recommendation by itself was enough to open any number of doors."

"Thank you. I was happy to help, but ..."

"No, really, Summer. It was an amazing reference. I'm sure that's why I got a second interview for the Invesco office manager job. And for the interview I have this afternoon at the medical school. Haven't heard from Invesco but even if nothing comes from it, it gave me interview experience, which is great and ..."

"If you'll let me get a word in edgewise here, I have something I want to say."

"I'm running off at the mouth, aren't I? Sorry. Go ahead."

"Yes, Darcy is coming back in ten days. But, no, telling you her return date wasn't the reason I wanted to talk to you. You know I think you've been a great addition to the company. You handle our clients well, you're a skilled office manager, and you're a good writer. Most importantly, you *get* what we're trying to do here." She sat back in her chair and smiled.

Bella was puzzled. Where was this leading?

"I don't want to lose you, but with Darcy returning, I can't really afford to keep you here. So, I have a proposal. You know how much trouble I've been having getting the branch office in Seattle off the ground. I've spent more time and money going back and forth between here and there than I ever thought would be necessary. I can't keep being an I-5 road warrior. But if I'm not there, nothing seems to move." She sighed and shook her head. "I didn't have this kind of trouble getting this office set up. It's making me crazy. The only thing I can think to do is to have boots-on-the-ground-eyes-on-the-prize oversight. Would you be willing to move there for however long it takes to get things settled? Head up the project for me?"

Bella was so stunned she couldn't make her mouth work. When she finally did, it was to say, "You'd trust me to be in charge of the whole thing?"

"There you go again. Your reaction is not the way to get a big promotion and a substantial raise, but yes, the general idea is you'd be in charge of the project. That's the good part. The downside is, I have no idea how long it will take to get it up and running. You could be there for the few months I hope it takes or the three years it looks like it might take at the rate things are going."

"I don't care. It would be an amazing opportunity for me. And the timing couldn't be better. The man who bought my father's house wants to terminate the rental agreement I have with him so he can take possession next month. I started apartment hunting last weekend. Now I'll just move my search to Seattle."

"So the answer's yes?"

"The answer is definitely yes."

"I'm delighted. I hoped you would be willing to take it on. Maybe between the two of us, we can figure out what needs to be done to get my branch office in Seattle off its ass." Summer stood, her hand extended. "Let's talk contract and salary this afternoon."

The reception's desk was only a short distance from Summer's office. Even so, after the conversation with her boss, Bella's legs were so wobbly from the shock of the offer she'd gotten she could barely make it back there. She dropped into the desk chair and stared across the room, not really seeing what was there, merely replaying the conversation in Summer's office.

No one ever had shown this level of confidence in her abilities before. Not her parents. Not her brothers. Certainly not the employees in the family real estate office who blew off any suggestions she'd made on how to do things differently, knowing she'd only gotten the job because she was related to the owners.

But Summer trusted her, was giving her a chance to prove herself. Summer was her hero. Heroine. Whatever. In the months she'd been running the office for BU/MU, Bella had rediscovered how good she was at organizing and managing a small business. More importantly, how much she liked doing it. She'd had a chance to hone her skills and grow her confidence. Not to mention use her writing skills.

Now, with this opportunity, she'd be able to show her brothers—and reinforce in herself—that she wasn't a spoiled brat with no goals, nothing to offer the world. Summer trusted her and she was beginning to trust herself.

All she had to do was find a place to live in Seattle and move her things there. After she sorted through all her parents' belongings, divided up the good stuff between her brothers, sold what no one wanted, and shipped what they did want to California, of course. Then she'd be ready to take on the challenge of figuring out what was going on with the Break Up or Make Up operation in Seattle.

Easy peasy.

•••

When she told her brothers about her new job, Bella was mildly offended although not terribly surprised when Carlos expressed his concern about her taking such a responsible position when she had no experience getting a business off the ground. Luis asked if she didn't think she was getting in over her head with such a challenge. Ernesto worried that she would be in a strange city without family around when she needed help, which he was sure she would. She was tempted to tell them to shove it but held her tongue. All their skepticism did was make her more determined to prove she could accomplish what Summer wanted done. She also kept to herself her secret hope—if she did a good enough job as project manager for this phase, she might have the chance to manage the new office when it opened up.

Her siblings' comments on her decision were followed by a series of e-mails in which they gave her unsolicited advice on everything from moving companies and how to pack glass art to which books to take to Powell's to sell and what papers needed to be shredded and which saved. Somehow, being on the way to proving herself made her brothers' interferences easier to take, and some of their advice was actually helpful.

For example, her brother Javier offered to make a couple calls to friends in the Seattle real estate business and ask for some advice on where she could find a safe, affordable place to live. Six months ago, she would have turned him down, so fed up with their interference she'd been. But now, her common sense told her to accept.

He put her in touch with Sandra Daniels, a woman she was sure was a former friend-with-benefits who hoped, by helping his sister, she'd revive the relationship with Javier. After a series of e-mails and texts with ideas on where to look for a place to live, she came to like the woman's sense of humor and was tempted to tell her Javier's track record made him a bad bet for a long-term relationship. But she couldn't bring herself to say hurtful things about her favorite brother or to make assumptions about a woman who might be someone she'd want to befriend when she moved.

After two weekends looking at all the listings Sandra sent her, she settled on a tiny but cozy one-bedroom apartment in an older building in the Fremont neighborhood. It was considerably smaller than the house she'd been living in, but it had the advantage of being all hers. At least it would be as soon as she got her parents' house cleaned out, made arrangements to move her things in, and got settled.

Tackling the problems with the BU/MU expansion was a little more complicated. She and her boss brainstormed for hours about how to hasten the glacial speed with which the process for changing the zoning was moving. Without the change, the house Summer had purchased couldn't operate as a commercial space and the renovations they'd planned couldn't be done.

The glitch in the process could all be traced back to a hostile neighborhood association president who seemed to think BU/MU was more akin to a brothel than a counseling service. The official was vocal in her opinion, which had resulted in bad P.R. in the local paper when the association formally objected to the project. Summer had put off hiring a Seattle business consultant to help with a marketing plan until the other problems got sorted out. It would be Bella's call when to bring MBA Consulting, the firm Summer had decided to hire, into the picture.

Since the new building didn't have the permits to open as a commercial space, Summer had been working out of a cubicle in an incubator building where the bare necessities of office life—a desk, phone service, and Wi-Fi—were provided. Bella would take over the space, as well as all the paperwork from the months of fighting every step of the way to get the business open, when she assumed the responsibilities Summer had entrusted to her.

Before she could leave Portland, however, she had to clean out her parents' home. It was much more emotionally difficult than she'd expected sorting through the treasures of their long life together. Some of the boxes she found in the basement were untouched from when her parents had moved from Southern California to be closer to her mother's one remaining sister. Sadly, because both of the women died within a month of one another less than a year after the senior Rodriguezes moved to Oregon, her father had never finished unpacking. She knew it was because he couldn't face the memories. It wasn't much easier for her to handle the same task.

She and her brothers agreed to divide everything in the house with Bella getting first choice, starting with her father's valuable art glass and first edition book collections. They also agreed to let her furnish her apartment in Seattle with what she wanted from the house. Letting her have first pick of the glass and books was a generous gesture. Letting her have the furniture was more out of disinterest than generosity. Her brothers' tastes—or that of their wives—didn't run to what had furnished a 5,000 square foot house for two old people, she was sure. She, on the other hand, had come to love some of the furnishings she'd been living with for several years, like the armoire in her bedroom, the wingback chairs and bookshelves from the living room, the tea wagon from the dining room. She was happy to have them. She'd sent photographs of all the remaining pieces to her four siblings, but so far not one of them claimed anything. Which probably meant she would have to sell it all before she left.

Dealing with everything made for long days. During the workweek, she was still helping out at BU/MU getting Darcy back up to speed on current clients and projects. In the evenings and on weekends, she packed boxes and sorted papers. But less than a month after she'd been offered the job, everything was finished. Her parents' house was empty and ready for the new owner. The furniture for her new apartment had been delivered; the rest had been sold. Papers and art were on the way to her brothers.

She was ready for Seattle.

Chapter Five

In one week, the partnership committee would hold its annual meeting and Taylor would be proposed for partnership. Nate Benjamin said the vote was pure formality. After all his hard work for the firm, Taylor was a slam dunk. Under other circumstances, counting the ways it could go wrong would have kept Taylor up nights worrying. But Nate's reassurance made him confident it would work out.

Besides, his worrying quotient had been pretty much used up by concerns about the consequences of something he'd rather thoughtlessly done at a citywide meeting of community activists three months earlier.

Using the bonus from his CloudCo deal as the down payment, Taylor had purchased a condo in Belltown. And wanting to be active in the management of the complex, he'd gotten involved in the homeowners' association. Volunteering to be the board's representative at the annual meeting of homeowners' associations from across the city seemed like a good way to get to know more about how other neighborhood associations worked.

Unfortunately, the meeting occurred right after he learned from Nate Benjamin, who had been contacted by Summer Olsen, about Break Up or Make Up's plan to expand into Seattle.

The news unsettled him, which had been something of a surprise. He'd been quite sure the whole Allison affair and how it ended were behind him. And he'd given up his plans for a targeted strike against Summer Olsen and her company, although he still considered her business foolish and lightweight and believed she, herself, was possibly the spawn of Satan.

In truth, he'd not thought of Allison much at all in the past months, having slowly come to realize what he'd felt when he'd read her stupid letter was less the pain of a lost love than a blow to his ego and disappointment at the failure of what he still considered a well-thought-out plan. He had faced the reality that the fondness he'd felt for Allison hadn't really been passion. When he was being honest about it, he had to admit she'd probably done him a favor by ending things. They had certainly looked good together, and they'd had a pleasant, if not particularly passion-filled, relationship. But just because she was a smart, attractive woman with the right qualifications for the job of wife didn't mean she was the love of his life. By leaving him, she'd made him realize he could have been about to marry a woman he liked quite a bit but was far from the perfect mate he'd been portraying her as.

No doubt the breakup had stung. It still did. A little, anyway. His pride had been battered, after all. But he had determined it was time to move on. It helped that he'd not run into her at any point since he got the letter, which, given they ran in the same small social circles, was something of a surprise.

He was still convinced the owner of Break Up or Make Up was related to at least one of the minor demons of hell, if not the chief devil himself, and her business had the dumbest name in the world. But her bad taste in business models and names wasn't his problem.

However, he'd been taken off guard when he heard Nate, at a partner's meeting, raving about a self-described (he was sure) "exciting new approach to business and personal relationships." If Nate had his way, Break Up or Make Up was not only coming to Seattle but would be coming to his office. Assuming his colleague would pull off acquiring them as a client, Taylor would have to hear the dumb name at every partner's meeting for the duration of whatever contract they signed with *her*. And he'd have to keep his opinions on the subject to himself for the same length of time.

The morning after he heard his firm was pitching Break Up or Make Up for work, and still thinking about what it might mean if his boss discovered he'd been the target of one of their infamous letters, he attended the fatal neighborhood association meeting.

He must not have had enough coffee before he went to the meeting. Or enough sleep the night before. Maybe he hadn't been thinking. Whatever the reason, when the president of the relevant neighborhood association where the new office was slated to open mentioned how another old house in their neighborhood had been sold to someone who wanted to change the zoning to commercial use, he found himself in a discussion about Summer Olsen's business.

It wouldn't have created a problem if he hadn't let drop that he'd heard some of their neighbors in Portland had issues with them. It wasn't a lie. He had, after all, actually talked to several adjacent residents and been told there was a parking problem. Of course, in Northwest Portland, saying there were parking issues was like saying it rained in the winter. But he didn't add that part.

However, in his conversation with the neighborhood official, his pointed questions made it sound, he decided afterward, more serious than it really was. He knew the residents of the neighborhood in which Summer had decided to locate her business didn't like having houses converted to commercial space. And he knew they had a history of objecting to zoning changes and building permits. Several times, the delays they'd caused had convinced a business to look elsewhere for space.

What he hadn't counted on was the speed with which the president of the neighborhood association had latched on to his casual comments and run with them. Right down to City Hall where she and her allies became the single biggest roadblock to the expansion of Break Up or Make Up. The company got a rash of bad press, the objections of nearby homeowners delayed the zoning change, and the permitting process ground to a halt.

If he'd planned it, Taylor couldn't have screwed up Summer's plans any better.

He tried suggesting to his friends in the planning department it was a flap over nothing, but they pointed out the obvious— once the ball of neighborhood objections started officially rolling, there was little anyone could do but wait for it to come to rest at the bottom of the hill. And the spate of bad press made this hill steeper and longer than usual. Nevertheless, Taylor urged the planner in charge of the project to look beyond the views of what he described as only a few neighbors and think about the need to encourage small businesses in the city. He did his best to sound convincing without revealing his role in starting the whole uproar. Because if he did, he was terrified he would lose the partnership he had worked so hard for.

It didn't seem fair. A couple offhand comments shouldn't undo years of hard work. Maybe after he'd made partner, he'd figure out a way to undo what he'd done. It was the only thing he could think of.

That and a determination to keep his mouth shut at neighborhood association meetings about anything other than the weather.

•••

Every time she drove to Seattle, Bella slowed down a bit to smile— no, *grin*—as she passed Boeing Field and the skyline of the city appeared in the distance. The view never got old. The Emerald City beckoned to her, as Oz had to Dorothy. All she needed was a dog, a tin man, a lion, and a scarecrow to make the fantasy real. Oh, and I-5 should be yellow brick and have only one lane.

The day she moved from Portland to her new home, her first glimpse of the skyline was even more exciting to her. There it was. The place where she'd make her new life. A beautiful city with impressively tall buildings and some of the most spectacular water views in the country. It was going to be fantastic.

But first she had to figure out the traffic and a whole new set of city streets on her way to her new residence. Not easy. Sandra Daniels had driven her to the apartment building when she'd originally seen it, and sadly, she hadn't paid attention to how to get there. Which left her at the mercy of traffic heavier than she was used to, but still going fast enough to make it hard to follow the Google directions she'd printed off before she left Portland. To make it more confusing, her phone's GPS was giving her different directions from the ones Google suggested.

She got off I-5 at the wrong exit, somehow got turned around, and wound up south of downtown at Safeco Field, which she recognized from having been to a baseball game there. She had no idea where her new home was in relation to the stadium. Finally she decided to ask a human being for directions. A kind convenience store owner told her how to get to her apartment.

Relief was mixed with excitement when she finally found the building. The familiar furniture, which had arrived before she did and was in place thanks to an understanding building manager, was comforting. The half dozen pieces of her father's art glass collection glowed in the late afternoon light and welcomed her. After moving some of the furniture in her living room around so it was exactly right and unpacking her clothes, she decided to treat herself to dinner at a little neighborhood café up the street. Tomorrow she'd fill the refrigerator and pantry. Then, the following day, she'd be ready to find her way to the incubator building where her cubicle—and her new job—awaited her.

• • •

Obviously, Bella was going to have to quickly get used to tangling with Seattle traffic. Luckily she didn't have a boss or a staff waiting for her on her first day in her new office because she badly underestimated the time it took to get from home to her cubicle.

Just as she'd found her new apartment eventually, she finally found her new work home. She spent the morning beginning to plow through a file cabinet of paperwork trying to get a handle on the project and its problems. The radio Summer had thoughtfully added to the bare bones office space helped. Bella discovered a new favorite music station and an amusing advice show to give her some background noise while she got up to speed on what Summer had faced trying to open her branch office.

It was unfortunate, really, that her boss was having all these difficulties. Bella had seen firsthand the kind of good work BU/MU and their roster of experts did for people. Having access to all the resources in one place was a blessing for people who were in stressful situations. While writing letters for people who felt unable to do it themselves, she had gotten to know so many nice people. There were sad stories, like the two lifelong best friends who were breaking up a home-based business because the spouse of one of the partners had embezzled money from the company to feed his gambling problem. His wife had known and covered for him. BU/MU's lawyers handled the business side, the psychologists the emotional part. Bella had written the letter to the offending partner from her childhood friend who'd been damaged, getting all her hurt feelings onto paper, freeing her to move on. Hopefully.

It wasn't all tragic stories and broken relationships, however. Sometimes she'd been asked to write fun, even funny, letters. There was the man who wanted a letter written to his neighbor's dog in the voice of his dog. It was a proposal of marriage—well, of mating, actually. It not only turned out to be successful but so funny a community newspaper picked up the story and gave BU/MU some free publicity.

Another favorite was the one she'd written for a twelve-year-old girl who asked for help with a letter to send to the boy she wanted to be her valentine. He was a ball boy for Portland's NBA team the Trail Blazers, and the girl saw him at every home game because she and her father had season tickets. The letter made the local news with both BU/MU and the Blazers getting television coverage.

Her favorite letters to write were the ones sent to make up after a fight, a separation, or counseling. They were always so hopeful. Often the clients came back with stories of success.

But now, she would be doing something much different and much more difficult. She'd been part of the team helping individuals to heal before. In this assignment, she was flying close to solo, helping to heal a business. She was determined to get a handle on what had derailed the expansion and get it back on track.

Chapter Six

"Welcome to Seattle, Bella!" Sandra Daniels set the basket she was carrying on Bella's desk. "I brought you a few essentials for life in your new hometown."

"You didn't have to do this," Bella said. She peeked through the cellophane wrapping on her real estate agent's gift. "But since the first two things I see are a 'Best Places Seattle' paperback and a Starbucks gift card, I'm not going to turn it away. I've been told this is the best guidebook for a new resident."

"It is. And if you can't find what you want there, call me and ask. I've lived here long enough to know how to find pretty much everything."

Bella pointed to the two mugs nestled in the basket bearing images of the Space Needle on them. "I just set up my brand new Keurig and would love to initiate it if you'd like a cup of coffee. I'll even turn off Dr. Sea-Tac so she doesn't interrupt us."

"So you've found Seattle's answer to Dr. Phil. I love her show. But I'll have to take a rain check on the coffee. I have a showing in about twenty minutes. I just stopped by to get the basket to you before you were no longer a newcomer." She hugged Bella. "Oh, one more thing before I leave. There's a Chamber of Commerce meet-and-greet tomorrow night at the Experience Music Project. Why don't you join me there, and I'll introduce you to a few people who might be able to give you some advice on how to get your project unstuck."

"I'd really appreciate the help. And I've always wanted to see what the building looks like inside. What time?"

"I'll be there about six thirty. See you then."

• • •

Normally Bella grabbed a skirt and blouse or a pair of pants and a knit top, found a jacket to go with it, and was out the door. Today, however, she couldn't make up her mind what to wear. She knew she was making a mountain out of something not quite so much a big deal, but she couldn't seem to stop herself from fussing. The Chamber meet-and-greet would be her first social occasion in Seattle, her first introduction to the business community, and she wanted to look right for it.

Four changes of clothes later, she decided to go with a black suit. The pencil skirt and long, hip-length jacket looked professional. The wide black belt and the soft, draped labels looked appealing. She thought it struck the balance she was looking for between serious professional and attractive woman. With a touch of caring and understanding. In a capable sort of way.

As if clothing could say all that.

Fortunately, she had a full day of dealing with city planners, potential consulting staff for the business, and a long conference call with Summer to distract her. She'd be able to forget her nervousness about walking into a room full of strangers and making a good impression. It had never been her favorite thing to do when she was working for her family business, and here the stakes were higher. She was representing Summer and a new business, the success of which would depend on acceptance in and cooperation from the community. And the latter hadn't been forthcoming so far.

At exactly six thirty, she walked into the Experience Music Project building, head high, with a purposeful stride. She was going to wow the Chamber of Commerce members no matter how nervous she was.

The setting helped. The Chamber of Commerce had picked a great place to have the business-after-hours reception. On a trip to Seattle with her father, she'd been intrigued when she'd seen the outside of the building. Designed by Frank Gehry, the architecture had been inspired by the deconstruction of a couple guitars. This event finally gave her a chance to explore the inside, a nice side benefit to her primary goal of networking with some of Seattle's movers and shakers.

By the time she arrived, the reception was already crowded. Standing about ten feet inside the entrance, she looked around. She didn't see Sandra but did locate the wine bar and headed there. When she eventually scored a glass of wine, she slowly walked around the room, looking at first for her acquaintance but caught almost immediately by the displays on the wall. She didn't pay attention to the people she was standing near until a familiar male voice said, "Bella? What on earth are you doing here?"

She turned suddenly enough to almost dump her drink on the man asking the question. "Marius. I should have known. I mean, I'm not surprised you're here."

"Yes, but I wouldn't have any reason to assume you would be." Marius Hernandez seemed more amused than annoyed, which was a relief, considering the last time she'd seen him she'd first hung all over him like kudzu then screamed at him for what she said was rude behavior when he didn't respond the way she wanted him to.

When she didn't immediately reply, he continued, "This would be the place where you tell me why you're here, since my family hasn't bothered to tell me you were anywhere near Seattle, let alone representing ..." He peered at the nametag she was wearing. "Break Up or Make Up, whatever that is."

"I'm sorry our families haven't been in better contact. A lot changed after my father died." She was sure the expression on her face showed she was still sad about her dad's passing. But this wasn't the time or place to get into the subject. She continued, "Actually, I've recently moved to Seattle. I'm in charge of opening the Seattle branch of a Portland company I've been working with the past few years."

"I didn't realize you'd been working in Portland, either. Sounds like we have a lot to catch up on. What does this company you work for do?"

"We work with clients who are negotiating difficult circumstances with personal or professional relationships. I started out writing for them and have moved up to management. It's an exciting opportunity."

"I'm happy you've found something to engage your talents. I know how rough it was for you after your father died."

Marius was the master of understatement. The son of one of her father's best friends, he had borne the brunt of her grab at security when she'd thrown herself at him trying to find someone to save her from dealing with the fallout from her father's death.

She had managed to convince herself that Marius was the answer to a prayer. He was handsome. His family and hers had known each other for generations. He'd even been the object of her teenage crush when she'd met him in Miami during a visit with relatives. Somehow, she was sure all she needed to do was flirt with him and he'd fall for her. It had worked with a couple other guys. Why not Marius?

Not only was it a bad idea to think about marrying someone only for security, but the man she'd picked was in love with a jewelry designer named Cynthia Blaine. Whom he was now married to. Which was almost a miracle considering how she'd spoken to Cynthia as she clung to Marius and demanded his attention.

"Yes, you do know." She cleared her throat and glanced at the ceiling before adding, "About that—I don't think I ever really apologized for my rudeness to Cynthia at the Art Museum that night. Has she ever forgiven me?"

He laughed. "Right now she's too busy with her jewelry designs and our daughter to worry about some random occurrence last year. There's no need to apologize. Or worry about it. Anyone who's ever lost someone they love would understand."

"Still, it was …"

"Awkward?"

"To say the least. I am sorry, Marius." She put her hand on his arm as she apologized when the thought occurred to her that his wife could be there and watching. Removing her hand, she asked, "Is she here tonight? I could apologize to her in person."

"She couldn't find a babysitter so she couldn't make it. Please, don't worry about it. It's water under the bridge." He took a sip of his wine before adding, "But if you're serious about talking to her, give me your phone number and address, and the next time we do something social at the house, I'll make sure you get invited and you can tell her yourself."

She wasn't sure what her reception would be at the Hernandez home, but she complied with the request. As she was scribbling her address on the back of a business card, Sandra Daniels joined them.

"I see you found my favorite coffee broker to chat up until I got here, Bella," she said as she put out her hand for Marius to shake.

"I'm the only coffee broker you know in Seattle, Sandra. And don't bother flattering me. Cynthia and I are still happy living where we are." His wide grin seemed to say he didn't really mean the dismissive words.

"Well, promise me you won't forget me when you're not. I'm sure I can sell that beautiful house of yours in a weekend." She looked back and forth from her client to the handsome coffee broker. "So, did you two know each other before you got here or …?"

Bella explained the family connections between the Hernandez and Rodriguez families, conveniently—or not so conveniently—omitting the event in Portland for which she had just apologized.

• • •

Who was the woman talking to Sandra and Marius? Taylor didn't think he'd ever seen her at one of these events before. If he had, he'd surely remember her. He'd never seen a more beautiful woman. Without her heels, she wouldn't be tall, not much over five feet, he thought, but a palpable energy emanated from her. He could feel it even across the room. Her long, dark hair was pulled back from her face in what looked like an attempt to tame wild curls that his fingers itched to touch, to see what they felt like. When she talked, as she was doing now, what he thought were dark eyes flashed, her lovely face was animated, and her hands participated in telling the story. She was about as far away from any woman he'd ever been attracted to as she could be, and yet he couldn't take his eyes off her.

Not only did she have a compelling face, but the rest of her was fascinating, too. Curvy hips were hugged by a slim skirt. Nicely toned legs showed from the hem right above her knees to a pair of sky-high heels. A fitted jacket emphasized a slender waist and a hint of cleavage. He hadn't been this fascinated by a woman in—well, he couldn't even remember when the last time was. He absolutely wanted to know more about her. As soon as he got a glass of wine, he'd go over and talk to Sandra and Marius. He knew both of them and could cadge an introduction from whichever of them knew her.

The crowd had grown enough that the line for the wine was twenty-deep. Taylor had almost decided to leave without a drink when a third bartender appeared and the line started moving faster. He stayed.

Big mistake.

By the time he got a glass of wine, the beautiful, dark-haired woman had disappeared into the crowd that had seemed to have doubled in size again during the time he'd been in line. He walked around the room, stopping at every small cluster of people, looking for her. Or Marius. Or Sandra. Both were also among the missing. Conversations with people he knew kept him from a laserlike focus on his quest, but after forty-five minutes of off and on searching, his glass was almost empty and he hadn't found any of the three people he was seeking. Sandra and Marius, he discovered in several conversations, had separately left. The woman, who'd intrigued him and who was unknown by anyone he talked to, had disappeared into the night like Cinderella. Without leaving a glass slipper or a phone number.

But Taylor had an advantage over Prince Charming. He didn't need a shoe to track his mysterious woman down. He had Marius Hernandez, whom he'd met when the coffee broker had used MBA Consulting's help in opening the Seattle branch of his family's business. As Taylor left the event after an hour more of socializing, he decided to call him on Monday. Surely Marius would know how to track her down.

Chapter Seven

"Taylor. It's been a long time," Marius said when he answered the phone. "It's good to hear from you. I hear you made partner at MBA. Congratulations. But if you're calling to see if I need your help again, I'm still implementing the ideas you gave me the last go around. Although I may have a name or two for you to call."

"I'm always ready to get the names of possible clients, but what I'm calling for is a favor." Taylor hesitated for a moment, suddenly wondering if his impulse would be interpreted as more like stalking than trying to get an introduction to an attractive woman.

"Just tell me what you want. MBA was the reason I had such a smooth entry into the Seattle business scene. Anything I can do for you, I will."

"Actually, it's a personal favor. And I'm beginning to feel a bit foolish asking."

"Personal, huh? That's interesting. Why don't you ask and let me decide if it's foolish."

"Okay. Look, it's about the woman you were talking to at the Chamber meet-and-greet the other evening ..."

"Which woman? I must have talked to a couple dozen or more. There was Tina Minor, she's a lawyer in town. And Sandra Daniels, she's a real estate broker. I'd have thought you'd know them. Then there was ..."

"No, she was a little brunette. In a black suit. You were talking to her when I walked in. It was about six forty-five or so."

"Ah, should have guessed."

Taylor swore he could hear a muffled laugh. "I know it sounds like something from middle school, but ..."

"You'd like to meet her."

"Yeah. I would. Do you know her well enough to arrange an introduction?"

"You could say so. We've known each other since we were kids. Her grandfather and mine came from Cuba together back in the early sixties. Her name is Isabella Rodriguez. She recently moved to Seattle. Opening an office for some company she's been working with for a while. Can't remember the name although I should. It's an odd one." There was a pause, as if he were trying to remember. "Doesn't matter. When you meet her, she can tell you. I'm sure she'd love to make new friends. She said she hasn't had much of a chance to meet people."

"Maybe you could ask her if it would be okay to give me her phone number. Or something."

"I have a better idea. Cynthia—my wife—is having a reception this coming Saturday at the Erickson Gallery. She's debuting some new jewelry designs for Max Erickson. I planned to invite Bella, and I'll see you get an invitation, too. I'll suggest she get there at seven. If you're there then, you can meet her. That work for you?"

"It's great. Thank you. I owe you."

"Actually not. It would be doing a favor for me to connect her with a few friends."

"Are you responsible for her or something?" Now Taylor was curious about the exact relationship between Marius and the lovely Ms. Rodriguez. Then a possibility occurred. "She's not an ex-girlfriend, is she?"

"God, no," Marius said before breaking into a loud laugh. "But please don't repeat your question in front of my wife."

"Is there a story there?"

"A long one. But it's too complicated for right now. Maybe some night over a drink, I'll tell you." Taylor could hear the rustle of paper. "Give me your home address so I can make sure Cynthia gets an invitation to you."

Taylor recited his mailing address, thanked Marius for his help, got the names of the leads for new clients, and disconnected the call. He'd succeeded in his goal of finding out who the beautiful woman was. Now all he had to do was figure out why it mattered to him so much.

•••

A week after the meet-and-greet, Bella was no closer to getting to the root of the problem with the zone change than she'd been the first day she arrived in Seattle. She'd talked to half a dozen people at the event who'd given her the names of people to contact in the city who might be able to give her some help or at least an insight into what was going on. She'd followed up on every one of the suggestions. But no matter whom she talked to, the story had been the same: the staff had flagged the application because of the formal opposition of the neighborhood association, and any action would have to wait until after a hearing. Which couldn't be scheduled for weeks, maybe as long as a couple months. If it took that long, Summer would miss her target date for opening.

The president of the neighborhood association who'd filed the objection was out of town so Bella couldn't talk to her. She did make an appointment with the city staffer who worked with the neighborhood associations, but he couldn't give her any better advice than anyone else had about how to get past the objections of the neighbors.

Bella was stumped. There was only so much work Summer was willing to pay to have the contractors begin in the house until after the zoning change was official, but what could be done, Bella got back on track. She was more successful at contacting lawyers, counselors, and writers who might be interested in joining their resource base, expanding their pool of expertise to provide the services the firm offered. She wouldn't be making the final decision about whom to work with, but she wanted to have the research done to discuss with Summer when she was next in Seattle.

She made the decision to move ahead with the marketing plan and set up a meeting with Nate Benjamin at MBA Consulting. Persuading Summer to stay overnight, she also scheduled a series of telephone and in-person interviews with the possible consultants she'd identified.

She felt reasonably satisfied with what she'd accomplished although her frustration at not being able to move the huge barrier of the zoning change bothered her. Maybe it was her lack of experience, maybe her concern she wasn't quite up to the challenge, but she was afraid she wasn't doing a good enough job and it ate at her confidence, in spite of Summer's continued praise for what she'd accomplished.

An invitation to a reception for Cynthia Blaine, Marius's wife, was a welcome distraction from her work worries. It came with a note from Marius asking her to be there by seven so he could introduce her to someone who wanted to meet her. As a chance to meet Cynthia at an event where they wouldn't be forced to carry on too much of a conversation but where she could apologize for her behavior a year ago, it was perfect. And she was curious about who could possibly know enough about her to want to meet her.

On the night of the event, she made sure to wear the neckpiece she owned created by Cynthia Blaine and left in plenty of time to get to the Pioneer Square gallery by seven.

It was the usual drizzly end-of-winter/beginning-of-spring night in Seattle, and finding a parking place was difficult, but on her third, or maybe fourth, swing around the block where the gallery was located, a car pulled out in front of her. She squeezed her little Kia into the space and ran through the rain toward the bright lights and buzz of the reception.

"How nice to see you." Marius greeted her with a hug as soon as she was in the door. She resisted at first because she could see, over his shoulder, the woman she knew was his wife. But when Cynthia smiled, she relaxed a bit and returned the gesture. He walked her across the gallery with his arm around her shoulders and stopped in front of his wife. Looking down at her, his expression one of barely contained amusement, he started the introductions. "Cynthia, you met Bella Rodriquez last year, but the circumstances weren't exactly the most conducive to getting to know each other." He couldn't seem to stop a wicked grin from breaking out. "Bella, I believe you remember Cynthia Blaine."

Bella could feel her face heat up with embarrassment.

"Oh, for heaven's sake, Marius, stop torturing the poor woman. Of course we remember meeting each other." Cynthia extended her hand. "We should both ignore my husband. He's having way too much fun with this. I'm happy you could join us tonight. It's long past time we met under more amiable circumstances. And you wore my Cleopatra collar Marius gave you."

"My *family* gave her, *querida*," Marius corrected.

"Sorry, your *family* gave her." The couple exchanged smiles, as if this was something they'd said to each other before.

Bella could feel the flush creeping up her neck again. "I love it. And I wear it all the time."

"I'm glad. I always like to know my pieces find homes with people who appreciate them."

"Can I get you a glass of champagne, Bella?" Marius asked.

"You don't have to. I can get my own," she said.

"No, you two talk. I'll be back shortly." Marius headed for the bar.

There was an awkward silence for a few moments. Bella broke it with, "I'm glad I have this chance to give you the apology I owe you for what happened in Portland at the art museum."

"That was some evening, wasn't it? Not exactly the best time for either of us," Cynthia said. "You'd just lost your father. I'd just found out I was pregnant and thought Marius was cheating on me."

"Yes, well, my hanging on to him like some sort of monkey certainly must have looked like he was. I'm sorry I upset you."

"Don't worry about it. Everything worked out. We're fine. So's our daughter. And you've got a great new job, Marius said."

"Yeah, I'm working on opening a branch office for a friend's business here in Seattle. I thought about contacting Marius when I moved here but wasn't sure what kind of reception I'd get after ... well, you know. Then I saw him at the Chamber event, and he was his usual friendly self."

"He was surprised his family hadn't mentioned you'd relocated. I assume your family knows you're here?"

"Yes, but since my father died, I don't know how much contact my brothers have with the Hernandez family."

"Well, I'm glad you could come tonight. Longtime friends like the two of you shouldn't lose touch, should they?"

Bella was impressed by how calm Cynthia seemed. Could she really be so understanding about the woman who'd tried to stake a claim to the man she was now married to? It seemed so. "You're being gracious and I appreciate it. I'm relieved we've begun to clear the air. But I shouldn't keep you from your other guests. Thank you for inviting me, by the way."

"No problem. The more the merrier at an opening reception. Besides, Marius said he'd invited someone who wants to meet you."

"Yes, he told me, although he didn't say who it was. Do you know?

Marius arrived with a flute of champagne before Cynthia could respond. "Here you are, Bella. And if you're asking about your secret admirer, no, he's not here yet. I expect him soon, however. When he gets here, I'll find you and make the introductions."

Two glasses of champagne, an hour, and at least five times around the gallery later, Bella decided to say her farewells and leave. She'd looked at Cynthia's work so many times, she was sure she could draw each piece from memory. And she was more and more convinced her mysterious admirer, whoever he was, had gotten cold feet. She didn't need to stay there any longer feeling rejected.

Marius tried to convince her to stay for a few more minutes, but she was tired of hanging around, waiting. She was beginning to feel desperate, too much like she'd felt the first time she'd met Cynthia Blaine, and she didn't like it.

When she begged off, Marius switched to asking her if he could pass along her phone number to the man. She asked him not to, unwilling to seem overeager, and slipped out into the dark, rainy night, headed for home.

Chapter Eight

Damn the traffic. Damn the parking around damned Pioneer Square. Most of all, damn the iBit executives for running hours over their allotted meeting time. Okay, maybe he shouldn't curse the hand that would be feeding him business and income for the foreseeable future. But as fascinating and important as the company was, the dinner meeting with them had gone on for far too long. And now he was stuck trying to find a place to park so he could get to the gallery with some hope of meeting Cinderella.

After fifteen minutes of having no parking karma whatsoever, he decided to double park and run into the gallery so Marius knew he was on his way and could keep Isabella from leaving until he could find a place to ditch his car. But before he could, a red car indicated it was about to pull out from the curb only a half block away from the gallery. Taylor flipped on his turn signal and waited for the driver to leave the space so he could park.

He knew as soon as he walked into the gallery he was too late.

"Where the hell have you been, Taylor?" Marius asked. "I kept her here as long as I could but she decided you'd changed your mind and left. Can't say I blame her."

"I know, I know. I'm sorry. I was at a dinner meeting with a new client and couldn't break away."

"You could have called. It might have helped convince her to stay."

"I did call. Twice. But you didn't pick up."

Marius pulled out his phone and checked the call log. "Oh, hell, you did. I forgot Cynthia asked me to turn my phone off so I wouldn't be distracted."

"Well, can you give me her phone number at least?"

"I asked her if it would be okay, and she said no. I think she was embarrassed."

"Oh, come on, Marius. Please?" He was begging, with no shred of pride. It wasn't like him, but damn it to hell, he'd decided he wanted to meet her and he always went after what he wanted with enthusiasm.

"Sorry, Taylor. I gave my word. What I can do is try to set up another way for you to meet her. Maybe a dinner party at our house or something. I'll have to check with Cynthia and work it out."

"I'd appreciate it, Marius. I *really* want to meet her."

"Yeah, I get it. I'll see what I can do." Marius clapped him on the shoulder. "Meantime, take a look around at my wife's work and have a glass of champagne."

Frustrated to have lost Cinderella again, Taylor wasn't in the mood for art or wine. So after a quick trip around the display cases, he left. If Marius wouldn't help, maybe Sandra Daniels could. She'd been talking to Isabella at the Chamber event, too. Even if she didn't know Isabella well, at least it was possible she knew how to contact her.

When he called Sandra the Monday after the gallery reception, he struck out there, too. Her assistant told him her boss was in Hawaii, but she took his phone number and promised to have her call when she returned.

After another week or so, when he didn't hear from either Marius or Sandra, he decided logic would dictate it was time to let go and move on. But for the first time in his life, logic wasn't doing the job of persuading him to let it go even though it should have been the signal that the amendment to his plan was right. Meeting someone hadn't been on his agenda at this point. After the breakup with Allison, he'd decided to take a year before getting involved with anyone again. He needed time to reassess his life plan, determine who would fit into it. The year wasn't up. He hadn't figured out what kind of woman he needed in his life so he had no idea if Isabella Rodriquez was whom he should be interested in.

But damn it, he had to admit he was unduly attracted to her in spite of the fact his taste usually ran to tall, cool blondes, not short brunettes.

As often happens—well, to everyone but Taylor who planned everything and didn't need help—by the time he'd almost convinced himself it was best to forget about Isabella, fate took over and gave him a different outcome than the one he expected.

He was in the process of packing up the last of his belongings from his old cubicle so he could move them into the office he'd finally been assigned as a new partner, one with a door and a view of the city street, when Nate Benjamin walked past. He was talking to two women. Apparently, from the bits of conversation Taylor heard, they were new clients. One woman, the person to whom Nate was directing his attention, was a tall, handsome blond with a winsome smile and a pleasant laugh. She was exactly the type of woman Taylor had always been attracted to.

But, instead, it was the other one who caught his attention. She was a short, dark-haired, dark-eyed knockout of a woman— Isabella Rodriquez had been delivered to his doorstep.

His memory of her curves had not been exaggerated, as he could see from the form-fitting skirt she wore with a soft looking shirt. He didn't really know much about what women's clothes were made of so he wasn't sure if it was silk. But he did know it draped nicely over her breasts, making them look inviting. The shoes she wore had heels moderate enough to be businesslike but high enough to emphasize her lovely legs and firm-looking bottom.

He stood up so fast he knocked both the chair over backward and a pile of papers off his desk. Without thinking, acting purely on impulse, he darted out of the cubicle to see the blond, his boss, and Isabella approach the small conference room where the partners often made pitches to new clients. He couldn't wait until they came out. He had to talk to her now.

Without thinking he called, "Isabella. Isabella Rodriquez. It's you, isn't it?"

She turned. "Yes, I'm Isabella Rodriquez." She cocked her head and frowned. "I'm sorry. Do I know you?"

Their gaze met and the sizzle was probably felt as far away as Mount Rainier. Taylor smiled and motioned to her to break away from the group. "Can I talk to you for a moment? Before you go into the conference room, I mean?"

Nate Benjamin interrupted. "Taylor, can this wait? We're about to have a meeting."

"It'll only take a minute. I promise," Taylor said. "I have to apologize to Isabella."

Nate looked confused. Shrugging his shoulders, he said, "I don't know what to say. He's not usually like this."

The blond woman glanced at him, then at Isabella. "What's this about, Bella? Do you know him?"

"No, I don't think so." She seemed to be considering what to do. Finally, she squared her shoulders, touched the blond's arm, and said, "But I'm curious. Give me a minute to see what he wants, and I'll join you."

She walked toward him, and the rest of the office fell away. All he could see was the gentle sway of her hips and the faintly puzzled look on her beautiful face. It was like the cliché scene in a movie where the lovers float toward each other across the meadow of wildflowers and fall into one another's arms. He could feel the heat of the summer sun, smell the earth and the faint scent of some blossom. He'd never believed those scenes were anything other than a screenwriter's fantasy. Now he knew otherwise.

...

She didn't know why she needed to find out what the man wanted, but she did. Maybe it was his looks. She'd always been attracted to dark-haired, dark-eyed men like the ones she'd grown up around. This man was neither. Yet from the moment they'd locked eyes, she could feel all the tingles accompanying a chemistry that excited her. And she could see in his eyes he felt it, too. His blue eyes had looked like the sky on a beautiful August day at first. But the closer she got to him, the darker they got.

His blond hair seemed to have a glow about it. All he needed was to lose his shirt and don a pair of shorts, and he'd be the picture of summer. And with the body he had—six feet something of well-toned male muscle from what she could see underneath his conservative Oxford cloth shirt, striped tie, and nicely fitting trousers—she wouldn't mind seeing him in nothing but a pair of shorts.

She never drooled over men. Never. But how could she avoid it when this one had the body of a young god and the face of an angel, if angels had sinfully sensuous mouths and the cheekbones of a male model? And his voice! Deep and soft, the kind you wanted to hear whispering in your ear while you ran your fingers through his thick, wavy hair, preferably when both of you were considerably less clothed than they were at the moment. The way he held himself and talked, he oozed confidence from his pores. He might not trace his family roots to the southern hemisphere, and he might not be able to *hablar Español*, but he was *muy sexy* nevertheless.

As soon as she was within handshake distance, he reached for her. "My name's Taylor Jordan."

"Hello. Apparently I don't need to tell you mine. You already know it." She took his hand and was startled. The sizzle she'd felt when their eyes met occurred again. When he didn't let go of her hand but rather covered it with his left hand and caressed her thumb with his, she was sure he'd felt it, too.

"Yes, your friend Marius Hernandez told me. I saw you with him at the Chamber of Commerce after-hours a couple weeks ago. When I couldn't find you in the crowd to introduce myself, I called him to ask for an introduction."

She shook off his hand, the sizzle replaced by her memory of how she felt when he didn't appear at the reception. "Oh, are you the man who never showed up at the Erickson Gallery?" She took a step back.

"Yes, and that's why I had to talk to you. To say how sorry I am I didn't make it in time to meet you. I was at a business dinner with a client, and it ran over. Way over. I got to the gallery less than five minutes after you left. Marius wasn't happy with me. And he said you weren't either. Rightly so. I couldn't persuade him to give me your number so I could apologize. I couldn't believe my luck when you walked past me a few minutes ago."

Nate Benjamin called from the door of the conference room, interrupting Taylor's apology. "Ms. Rodriguez, we're about to start the presentation. Taylor, finish this up after our meeting." She could tell from the tone of his voice he was losing patience.

"I have to get to the meeting." She wasn't sure why, but she wanted to give the man a chance to explain further. "Will you be around in an hour or so?"

"I'll make sure I am. My office is the second one on the right, straight ..."

"Second star to the right and straight on 'til morning?"

"I beg your pardon?"

"Sorry. I guess you don't know *Peter Pan* as well as I do. I'll find you after my meeting. I promise."

She walked back down the hall to the conference room where her boss waited, feeling quite sure the young blond god was watching her every step. Hell, yes, she'd find him after the meeting. She had to find out if he was sincere or if he was only trying not to offend Marius. God knows, she hoped he was for real. She hadn't met anyone as attractive as this man in a long, long time. It would be a shame if he were only apologizing because of a business connection.

• • •

Taylor sat at his desk, a box of office supplies in front of him, which he was supposed to be stashing in his new cherry wood desk. Instead, he was looking up at what felt like ten second intervals to see if Isabella had appeared at the door of his office. Jesus, Nate was right. He never behaved like this. What the hell was he doing? What happened to the plan to swear off women for the foreseeable future? Or at least until he figured out what kind of woman he wanted to fit into his life.

No, here he was mooning around like a lovesick teenager with his first crush. Over a woman he knew nothing about other than her grandparents came from Cuba and they had a friend in common. Oh, and she was beautiful. The worst part was, in spite of knowing nothing about her to assure him she'd fit into his plan, he didn't care. He knew he had to convince her to go out with him.

The next hour was probably the most unproductive of Taylor's entire career. He kept looking out at the conference room where Isabella was meeting with Nate and the blond, checking the time on his computer or listening for her voice coming down the hall. So busy was he with those activities, all he got accomplished was to figure out where he wanted to keep paperclips and rubber bands. Oh, and he set the password on his new laptop.

Finally he heard Nate's voice out in the hall saying, "Great. I think I have a clear idea what you're looking for, and I know we can deliver something you'll find useful."

A woman's voice, the blond he was sure, said, "I loved the ideas you talked about. How soon do you think you'll have something for me ... for us ... to look at?"

"Maybe in a week, ten days, if that time frame works for you."

"More than works." Her laugh didn't have much humor in it. "At the rate we're progressing on this project, you could probably take ten weeks and we'd be okay."

Nate said, "Maybe we can give you some help with the problems you described, too. Let me give it some thought and see what I can come up with."

"If you can give me some advice on how to get a project unstuck, I'll be your fan for life."

Even Taylor could hear the smile in Nate's voice. "If that's the reward, I'll work on your stuck project problem first. I can always use another fan."

For God's sake, Nate, Taylor thought, *quit flirting and walk them to the reception area so I can have a chance to talk to Isabella.*

But just as he was about to go into the hall, the trio walked past him. Nate and the blonde kept walking, seeming not to miss the third member of the group who had stopped and was standing at the door of his office, smiling at him.

"How'd your meeting go?" Taylor asked.

She took two steps into his office. "Really well. Nate had some amazing ideas."

"He's a marketing genius."

"Easy to understand."

The ensuing silence was broken when both of them started saying, "I was wondering ..."

Taylor waved his hand as if encouraging her to speak ahead of him. "Ladies first."

"I was wondering ... maybe we could, I don't know, have coffee or something."

He glanced at the clock on his computer and groaned. "I'd love to. But I have a client meeting in ten minutes."

"Oh. Well, maybe another time."

He was happier than he should have been at the disappointment in her voice. "But I don't know where to reach you, remember?"

A smile appeared as she said, "I'll give you my card. Call me when you have time for coffee or lunch ... or something."

He took the business card she'd dug out of her messenger bag and stuck it in his trouser pocket. "Oh, and I apologize for babbling when you first got here. It was the surprise. Of seeing you, I mean."

"Don't apologize. I was flattered." She touched his hand, and the sparks ignited again. Damn, the woman was amazing. "I better catch up with my boss. She's got the car keys. I'll look forward to hearing from you."

After he watched her disappear into the reception area, Taylor went back into his office and dropped into his desk chair. He wasn't exactly proud of how he had handled the whole interchange. He'd barely gotten out with his dignity intact, all because Isabella Rodriquez was the most attractive woman he'd met in forever. Her smile warmed parts of his heart he didn't even know had been cold. And her body reminded other parts of him what it was like to be alive and aroused. He was sure she'd figured out how attracted he was; he'd been that obvious. But he didn't care. Nor did he care he was violating his plan not to get involved with anyone for a while. Not to mention his rule about not dating clients. All he cared about at the moment was figuring out how long to wait to call her.

Call her. Her card. He needed to get it out of his pocket before he lost it or it got sent to the dry cleaners or something. He pulled it out and glanced at it. The logo, a heart with fancy script letters over it, looked vaguely familiar. She must work for a company he knew from someplace.

Then he read the text and swore. Goddamn son of a bitch.

No wonder he recognized the logo. Her card said she was a project manager for Break Up or Make Up, the company he'd blamed—in front of witnesses, even—for wrecking his relationship with Allison. The most beautiful woman he'd met in years worked for the demon-in-chief, Summer Olsen. Then another reality dawned. The blonde with Isabella, the one she said was her boss.

Summer Olsen in the flesh.

Not only did Isabella work for her but now so did his firm. MBA was about to create a marketing plan to make Summer Olsen's company successful in Seattle. And there wasn't a damn thing he could do about it. The irony didn't escape him. He was a partner. Some of his income would come from the company that had badly battered his pride.

Even worse, all his plans to inveigle Isabella Rodriguez into a date would have to be put on ice. He had to erase any thought of how good being with her could be. If he didn't, he'd have to face his own foolish behavior in her boss's office every time he looked at her, as well as admit to her what he'd started with his offhand comment to the neighborhood association president. Even if he'd gotten past the letter Allison had sent him, and he was reasonably certain he had, he still had all the embarrassment and guilt of those two things to contend with. He'd almost been willing to break his rule of not dating clients for her, but this client carried a whole lot of other baggage.

No, he'd better stick with the plan the way he'd originally set it up. Isabella Rodriquez was off limits.

Damn it.

Chapter Nine

Summer had parked a couple blocks away from the MBA offices, and it was raining so the sprint to the car made conversation difficult. But once they were settled and Summer had pulled out into traffic, she started the cross-examination.

"Okay, spill. Who is he? Where did you meet him? What did he want? When are you seeing him?"

Bella laughed. "Slow down. His name is Taylor Jordan. You saw where I met him—in the hall of MBA Consulting."

Summer glanced over at her and shook her head. "Oh, come on. He knew who you were. I don't believe you just met him. I saw the way he looked at you. And the way you're blushing now."

"I said *I* met *him* there. I didn't say that's where *he* met *me*. Or at least where he saw me. Remember the Chamber of Commerce thing I went to a few weeks ago? He saw me there with an old family friend, Marius Hernandez, who ..."

"Was the one you threw yourself at after your father died. Right?"

"Thank you for reminding me of my humiliation."

"Isn't that what friends are for?"

"Do you want to know about Taylor or not?"

"Sorry. Finish."

"Anyway, he called Marius and set up a way to meet me at the Erickson Gallery."

"Oh my God! He's the guy who stood you up."

"Again, thanks for the reminder of my humiliation."

"Give it a rest, girlfriend. He's clearly interested. There must have been a good reason."

"He was held up in a dinner meeting, he said, and arrived at the gallery right after I left. I could check it out with Marius, but

I believe him. Anyway, the reason he practically chased me down the hall today was to apologize for not getting to the gallery on time."

"He couldn't have called you and apologized?"

"I asked Marius not to give him my number."

"So? What now?"

"He has my number now, and he says he'll call. I hope he does. He's well, he's ... I don't know. He's ... how can I put it? Maybe blond Viking god works. Or 'wow.'"

"His boss is pretty 'wow,' too, don't you think?"

"I guess." She smirked at Summer. "Assuming you think tall, dark, and handsome with a sexy voice and jade green eyes is 'wow.'"

"Keep your attention on the Viking. The green-eyed one is mine."

Bella had already been excited about moving to Seattle for work reasons. Now, Taylor Jordan gave her a whole other set of reasons to love her new job and her new city. He was hot. If he was a partner at MBA, he was smart, too. It had been a long time since a man had interested her like this.

She had a good feeling about meeting him today.

• • •

Two weeks later, Bella was beginning to doubt her optimistic feeling. Taylor hadn't called. She'd been so sure he would. The signs were all there. She might not be the most experienced woman in the world, but she knew what it felt like when a man was attracted to her. And what it felt like to be attracted to a sexy man.

Maybe he was out of town on business. Or maybe he had a girlfriend. She hadn't seen a ring on his left hand so she'd assumed he wasn't married, but he could have a significant other. He didn't seem like the kind of man who'd try to meet someone when he already had a girlfriend, but you never knew. Marius wouldn't fix her up with someone who was already taken, would he?

Unless he didn't know.

The whole thing was driving her crazy. How was she going to find out why he wasn't calling? Maybe Summer could ask Nate. He'd know if Taylor was out of town. Or taken.

No, she was being silly. Asking Summer to ask Nate was too much like middle school where you ask your friend to ask a friend if Bobby or Billy likes you before you ask him to hang out with you at lunch.

Luckily, an opportunity to do her own reconnaissance fell into her lap.

Summer had forwarded a packet of information to her from MBA that included the marketing plan Nate had promised, as well as suggestions he had for straightening out the mess with the zoning variance. She asked Bella to review it, read the comments and suggestions she had made, and add her own take on it. The material was in hard copy instead of an e-mail because the infographics he'd included were easier, Nate had written, to see on paper than on a computer. When she was finished, she was supposed to return it to MBA with her thoughts. Summer had even enclosed an addressed, stamped envelope for her to use. But she decided she'd rather give Nate her input in person. Late one Friday afternoon, after she spent two days going over the marketing plan and writing a memo with her comments, Bella called to see if Nate had some free time. When she was told he was in all afternoon, she headed for the MBA offices.

One way or the other, she was going to find out what was going on with Mr. Taylor Jordan.

Who wasn't in his office when she arrived. Nate was waiting for her, however, and seemed genuinely pleased to discuss the questions and comments she and Summer had about his work. They reviewed everything and hammered out a few more details.

She was about ready to leave when the door to Nate's office opened and Taylor came in.

"Nate, I've got a problem I need ..." He seemed to suddenly see his colleague wasn't alone. "Oh, sorry. I didn't realize you had someone with you." He nodded but didn't smile as he acknowledged her. "I apologize, Isabella. I didn't mean to interrupt your meeting. I'll come back." He turned to leave.

He was as good looking—as sexy—as she remembered him, damn it, but from his reaction, he was much less interested in seeing her than he had seemed the last time she'd been in the office. Guess her question had been answered—she was more interested than he was, in spite of his chasing her down the hall the last time she'd been in the MBA office.

Nate rose from his desk. "Hang on. You're not interrupting anything. We were about finished. And I was just talking about you." He turned to her. "I think I can incorporate all the comments and suggestions you and Summer made into the plan in the next couple days and e-mail the text to you both. I don't think the infographics will change, so why don't we save a tree and do it electronically this time?"

Taylor continued to edge his way to the door, avoiding her eyes. "You need to get your business wrapped up. I can do this later," he said.

Nate was persistent. "No. Don't leave. What we were talking about, other than that last bit of business, was Bella's appalling lack of exposure to anything fun in Seattle. She hasn't done much except work since she moved here. I told her she needed a local guide to show her around. You up for helping out with her dilemma?"

Of all the things she needed, a fix-up with Taylor by his senior partner would be the last. "No one has to be my guide," she protested. "I'm perfectly capable of finding the Space Needle by myself."

"I'm sure you are, but there's more to Seattle than the Space Needle. Wouldn't you agree, Taylor?"

For some reason, Nate was determined to make this work although she had no idea why.

"How about you walk Bella out to the elevator and see if you can interest her in engaging your services?" Nate said. "Then come back so we can take care of whatever it was you wanted to see me about."

The look of discomfort on Taylor's face said volumes about how unenthusiastic he was about the suggestion Nate had made.

"I also know where the elevator is," Bella said. No way was she going to force herself on him, even for a short walk down the hall. Boy, had she misjudged his interest. She'd been off by a mile if the cool control he was now showing was any measure. It must have been something other than personal attraction she'd sensed. Maybe he'd seen her as a business opportunity. She wasn't experienced with the ins and outs of how consultants marketed their services. Maybe they chased them through mutual friends.

But that didn't make any sense either. She didn't think he'd known who she worked for until he'd met her in his office, and by then, her company was already a client of his firm.

It didn't matter. She'd been wrong. And it was only too clear right now. Look at the way he was frowning and avoiding her eyes. He looked like he'd been asked to take a long walk off a short pier.

However, he was a loyal partner in MBA apparently because in response to his colleague's request, he straightened up, opened the door all the way, and said, "Of course I can walk you to the elevator, Isabella."

She shook Nate's hand and thanked him for his time. She heard Taylor say, "Back in a minute," as she walked as fast as she could to the reception area and the elevator bank.

They stood in silence after she pushed the "down" button. It seemed to be taking forever for the car to arrive. Either time really was relative and was now dragging, or all the cars were on other floors being loaded with all the people and/or furniture on one floor so it could be delivered to another floor, totally bypassing where Taylor and Bella were waiting.

It was torture. Something had to give, and it was apparently not going to be Taylor. So, finally, she spoke. "I want to go over the revisions Nate and I talked about while our conversation is still fresh in my mind. I don't feel like going back to my cubicle. Is there someplace downstairs I can hang out and read for a bit? Maybe a coffee shop or a bar?"

"There's a bar on the ground floor. Most of us in the building go there from time to time. They even have decent food."

"Sounds perfect. It'll take me an hour or so to go over the changes we made and try to figure out what my next steps should be to get this project on track." On an impulse that started her mouth moving before she could stop it, she added, "If you'd like to join me, I'll buy you a glass of wine."

The invitation was no sooner out than the elevator arrived and she got in, not waiting for Taylor to respond. Her legs were shaking; her mouth was dry. She couldn't look him in the face. She had no idea why she'd been so bold. No idea if he'd show up. But the ball was in his court. This would show her once and for all if she'd been wrong about his interest.

Chapter Ten

Taylor watched the door of the elevator close but said nothing in reply to Isabella's invitation. He didn't know what, exactly, he should say. He knew what he wanted to *do*—in spite of knowing whom she worked for, in spite of swearing it wasn't the right time and she wasn't the right woman, he still felt the same electricity when she looked at him as he'd felt the first time they'd locked eyes. It was so powerful he wanted to run down the steps and beat the elevator to the first floor, grab her when she got out, and kiss her.

But he couldn't. All the reasons he had outlined to himself over the past two weeks on an almost daily basis were still valid. It didn't matter how attracted he was to her. There were too many things working against them, not the least of which was if she ever found out who he was and what he'd done, she'd either laugh at him or flat out hate him.

No, this wasn't how he operated. He needed a nice, safe, appropriate woman who would go with him on nice, safe, appropriate dates, which would progress to a place where he could make a nice, safe, appropriate decision about what to do with the relationship. It was how he'd always assumed he'd find a wife.

Right. Look how well it had worked out with Allison. So well, he'd sworn he'd take time off before returning to his plan for finding a wife.

And he couldn't let Isabella Rodriquez mess it all up. Could he?

His musing was interrupted by a woman's voice asking him if he was getting on the elevator or not. From the tone of her comment, it wasn't the first time she'd asked. He apologized, told her he wasn't getting on, and, with a determined stride, went back to his office. Work was the answer. He'd bury himself in his projects and forget about those big brown eyes, the soft, dark curls, and her seductive smile.

When he saw the folder in his hand, he remembered what he'd wanted to talk to Nate about and, with a relieved sigh, tracked him down, intending to spend a few minutes discussing the details of a report he was responsible for writing.

It didn't go as he planned.

He had no sooner walked into Nate's office than his colleague asked, "Well? Did you set something up?"

"Set *what* up?"

"Taking Bella around the city."

"Were you really serious? I thought it was company policy not to date clients. And if that's not the case, why don't you show her around Seattle?"

Ticking his points off on his fingers, Nate said, "One, I was serious. Two, there's no company policy about dating clients, you've just never done it. Three, she's not your client, she's mine. Four, Bella's new in town, all alone, and hasn't had a chance to do much of anything except work. Five, I'm in the middle of a messy divorce and custody battle and can't afford to be seen with a beautiful woman. Six, oh, hell, I have to move to a second set of fingers."

"Okay, okay. I get your point. But since when are we an adjunct to Grey Line tours?"

"Don't be such an ass, Taylor. You've been sulking ever since what's-her-name broke it off with you. It's time you got back in the game. And Bella's an intelligent, beautiful woman who could use a friend. Can't you do even one spontaneous thing and just take her around the city?"

"I do spontaneous things all the time."

"Yeah, right." He reached for the folder Taylor was holding. "Never mind. I give up. But it was worth a shot. What do you want me to look over?"

When they were finished reviewing the report, Taylor went back to his office and tried to focus on getting what they'd discussed onto his computer. It didn't work. All he could see were those big brown eyes looking at him so hesitantly from the back of the elevator after she'd put herself out there and asked him to join her for a drink. He knew she'd be disappointed if he didn't show up. But he knew she'd be even more disappointed if she ever found out the truth about him.

Finally, after almost an hour of doing absolutely nothing except going over yet again the reasons he shouldn't pursue Isabella Rodriquez any further, he decided to get the hell out of Dodge. Once he got home, he wouldn't have to think about what kind of temptation she posed. Or, at least, he hoped he wouldn't.

Waiting for the elevator, he continued his little internal pep talk. All he had to do was walk out the door and get the bus. He'd get home in no time at all. He had leftover Chinese in the refrigerator and dozens and dozens of choices on his TV. Or he could browse Netflix and watch a movie. He'd simply immerse himself in mindless programming. There. Easily done.

First, of course, he had to get past the Conference Room, the bar run by a former public relations guru and frequented by most of the tenants in the building. He wouldn't glance in. Wouldn't look to see if Isabella was there. She was probably gone by now. She wouldn't hang around waiting for him when it was obvious he wasn't going to show up. He had nothing to worry about.

He got to the first floor and couldn't seem to take more than a step or two away from the elevator, frozen in place by the sudden fear she *had* waited for him. She *would* be sitting in the bar. She'd look up with her sweet smile when she saw him, and he'd be toast.

Maybe he should take the back way out of the building so he wouldn't have to pass the bar and be lured in.

The mumbled curses of the people trying to exit the elevator broke through his obsessive musings. He knew he was being a pain in the butt, but his feet refused to move closer to the front exit. He murmured apology after apology as the crowd surged out, more eager than he was to get to the door.

After the door to the elevator closed, he finally moved, planning to give a wide berth to the bar. But as he reached a spot opposite the bar's glass wall looking out on the lobby, he decided it wouldn't hurt to take a little peek inside. To make sure Isabella was okay. If she was there. Not that she would be. She'd have long since gone home.

But she hadn't. There she was. Seated at one of the small cocktail tables, she had a half-full glass of wine in front of her as well as a sheaf of papers. Chewing on a pen in one hand, with the other, she was twisting a curl around her forefinger. A slight frown created a crease between her eyes, a crease he wanted to erase with the pad of his thumb. She looked ... cute was the word that came to mind. Cute and adorable. Not the usual words he'd use to describe a woman he was attracted to, but they were the only words he could think of at the moment.

Well, sexy, too. The table was small. He could see her slender legs crossed under it. With the foot not on the ground, she was bouncing her completely inappropriate red shoe on the tips of her toes. It was mesmerizing to watch. Twist the curl. Bounce the shoe. Twist the curl. Bounce the shoe.

This time his feet wouldn't stop moving but took him straight to the table where she was sitting. When she looked up and saw him, a smile lit up her face and warmed him all over.

"You came. I wasn't sure you would." She indicated the chair opposite her. "Can I get you a glass of wine? A drink?"

He dropped to the chair and shrugged off his raincoat. "Ah, sure. That would be great."

"Which?"

"Which what?"

"Which do you want—a glass of wine or a drink?"

"Whatever you're having is fine."

She looked around for the server, caught his eye, and indicated they needed another glass of wine. "So, did you get your problem sorted out with Nate after I left?"

"Yes, of course. But before we get to the small talk, can I explain something?"

"What do you need to explain?"

"I imagine you think I'm some sort of nut case, the way I chased you the last time you were in the office then ignored you today."

"I'm not sure I'd describe it that way, but it did seem a bit... ... well, maybe odd is the best word."

He could feel his face flushing slightly. It made him uncomfortable. He never blushed. How the hell did this woman put him so far off track? "I'm not sure how to explain. Where to begin."

"The beginning is usually the best place."

"I guess the beginning is, I'm a very organized person. I plan everything carefully. It's how I get things done. How I feel comfortable."

The server interrupted with his glass of red wine.

"Anyway, I've always been careful about my social life. The relationships I've had with women are usually based on friendship or a business connection. Never an across-a-crowded-room meeting. I've never in my life chased a woman the way I chased you after seeing you in a crowd."

"I'd hardly say you chased me."

"It feels like I did. I saw you. I wanted to meet you. I tracked you down. It's as close to stalking as I'm likely to get." He took a large gulp of liquid courage.

Although she smiled as she said it, when she commented, "I've never much liked the idea of being stalked," he frowned. Had she objected to his attention? His expression must have registered with her because she quickly added, "But I didn't feel stalked. Really."

"Seriously? I think that's close to what I did. Calling Marius? That's not me. Showing up at an art gallery to meet someone I don't know? I've never even had a blind date because I don't like the uncertainty of it." The stem of his wine glass suddenly seemed of infinite interest requiring him to study it carefully.

"Well, technically, you're still safe there because you didn't show up on time for the fix-up." She was making fun of him, he was pretty sure.

"Yes, well, that's another thing out of character. I'm never late for anything."

He paused before looking up from his glass. "Then, I've always had a policy not to date my clients. It's too complicated. Too likely to interfere with doing good work." He drank about half of the wine left in his glass. The alcohol was making it easier to be honest with her. "And my job… … my career… … has always been the most important thing in my life."

"And it shows. According to Nate, you made partner sooner than anyone in the history of the firm."

"Yes, it's true." He couldn't figure out why Nate would have told her that. "How did the topic of my partnership come up in conversation?"

"I asked about you." She raised an eyebrow at him and laughed. "Don't look so surprised. Surely you noticed what happened when we shook hands. I'm not immune to chemistry. I hoped you weren't either. So I asked about you."

"What else did he say?"

"Not much. He said told me you work with tech firms and small start-ups. Said you were hellishly smart. He didn't warn me off you by telling me about some company policy about dating clients, although he did tell me you were unattached at the moment."

"Well, it's not official company policy. It's unofficial, I guess you can say."

She leaned across the table and touched his hand.

"Taylor, I'm not your client. My boss is your boss's client."

"Technically, Nate and I are equals because we're both partners."

"But you still think of him as your boss, don't you?"

"Yes. How did you know?"

"The way you relate to him. Let's get back to the unofficial official policy of not dating clients. Do you really mean it?"

"I don't know right now. I guess I think it's the right approach most of the time, but maybe there should be some exceptions." He wasn't sure which was muddling his mind more, the alcohol or the warmth of her touch.

When he didn't continue with an explanation of what those exceptions might be, she shook her head. "Okay, let me see if I have it right so far. In a nutshell, what you've told me is, you've never been attracted to someone without a plan in mind for the relationship, so when you felt this chemistry ... and please tell me you feel the same chemistry I do ..."

She waited for him to nod before continuing. "So, you were wrong-footed by feeling this chemistry without a plan, then undone when you found out I was a sort-of client, which is, I am to assume, the reason you didn't call. And today, in spite of all that, you debated for approximately ..." She looked at her phone. "Approximately fifty-nine minutes about whether you should come down to the bar to meet me."

She smiled at him, a bit wistfully, he thought. "I'd even go so far as to say you probably hesitated when you got to the bar door, trying to decide if you should come in. And now you're trying to rationalize sitting here with me by thinking up some exception to a rule that really doesn't exist even though you obey it." She shrugged. "Have I about covered it?"

"It didn't sound quite as absurd when I was thinking about it, but, yes, I guess you have." He finished his glass of wine. "You're not at all like anyone I've ever met."

"That makes me happy." This smile crinkled her eyes in a most appealing way. "I like being different from other people in your life." She waved to the server for their bill.

"Let me." He reached for the check as soon as the waiter put it on the table.

She moved it away from his hand. "Nope. I asked you here. I pick up the tab. Besides, one glass of wine is hardly worth arm-wrestling over, is it? You can pay for dinner."

He wasn't sure he heard her correctly. "Dinner?"

"Yes, you know the meal you eat in the evening. Sometimes even with someone you think might be good company."

"Ah, yes. Dinner." It took a moment for it to sink in. "Right. Dinner. You mean tonight? You and me?"

"Yup."

"Okay, I'll get dinner. There's a French bistro I like a couple blocks from here. Sound good to you?"

He wasn't sure if she was having second thoughts or was stunned when she didn't answer right away. "Wow," she eventually said. "That was easier than I thought it would be. I was thinking I'd have to put up a fuss to get you to ask a client to dinner, it being against your rules and all."

"I thought you said you weren't a client. But even if you are, you were the one who did the asking, weren't you? So, technically, I didn't make the request. I was invited."

"Let's not get hung up on details." She signed the credit card receipt the server put in front of her. "I'm hungry. I have no plans for dinner, and I'd like to continue this conversation." She rose from her chair and handed him her raincoat so he could help her put it on. "You interest me, Taylor Jordan. I want to find out what makes you tick. So, however you parse the words, we're having dinner together and you're paying for it."

As they walked out of the building, the same stupid second thoughts wormed their way into his mind. He was going to have to work hard to keep her from doing what she said she wanted to do. If she ever found out *everything* about him, he was doomed. Yet he couldn't seem to keep himself from wanting to spend time with her. He didn't know what the hell was going on—all he knew was he both wanted to be with her and thought he shouldn't. So far, tonight, the wanting was winning.

• • •

Bella didn't know what had come over her. She'd never flirted so obviously with any man. Had never had to. She'd spent most of her life since adolescence being the flirt-ee, not the flirt-er. The interchange with Taylor showed she liked turning the tables.

Six months ago, she'd have never thought to declare her interest in getting to know a man or asking him to take her to dinner. Without a doubt, her time with Summer and BU/MU had built her confidence, made her a stronger and more self-reliant woman. She'd assumed the sense of purpose she was developing would be reflected primarily in her professional life. But she was wrong. It seeped into her personal life, too. Like tonight. When she took a chance and got what she wanted—dinner with Taylor Jordan and a chance to see if he was as interesting up close and personal as he was at first meeting.

As a bonus, she was in a restaurant she'd never have found on her own. As soon as they walked in, she knew it would be good. The smell of something delicious made her realize how hungry she really was. She decided to let him order and wasn't disappointed with his choices. He asked for a bottle of a Northwest pinot noir and a charcuterie platter, laden with interesting cuts of sausages and pâtés. Then their server brought a large plate of melted raclette cheese with potatoes and pickles on the side. She not only liked the food, she loved he had ordered only things to share.

Conversation over dinner came more easily than she expected, given the rather awkward circumstances of their being together. They talked a little about where they grew up and went to college. He waved off any talk of work, which she assumed was because of his "no client dating" rule. It was when he asked if Nate's comment was correct about her having done or seen nothing other than work since she moved to Seattle, that things got interesting.

"I'm afraid he wasn't exaggerating. If it's not in my apartment, my cubicle, or the MBA office, I haven't seen it," she confessed. "I've been so busy trying to sort out what's going on with the expansion, I haven't had much time to find out what's going on in the city."

"You haven't been to the Pike Place Market?"

She shook her head.

"The outdoor sculpture garden?"

Another head shake.

"Ridden a ferry? Gone to the symphony? Visited The Museum of Flight?"

"No, no, and no."

"As a native of the city, I'm appalled. You're missing out on the real reasons to live in Seattle. If you don't enjoy things like that, all you're left with is rain and traffic congestion."

She laughed. "I certainly didn't mean to let down the locals. I promise I'll ride the monorail and get myself to the Space Needle soon."

"It's touristy and there are other places more interesting, although the view of the city from there is pretty spectacular." He scooped up the last bit of cheese from the platter. "I think Nate's right. You need a tour guide to show you around."

"Do you know anyone who's qualified?" She was hopeful she knew where this conversation was going, but she fought hard not to have her face show it.

"Yeah. Me. What are you doing tomorrow?"

"You don't have to give up your Saturday because Nate made a silly comment. And what about that rule of yours?"

"First of all, I'm not volunteering because of Nate. I've enjoyed tonight. I think it would be fun to show you around tomorrow. Second, I'm not dating you. I'm acting as your tour guide to introduce you to the city I love."

"Of course. Sorry. How could I have possibly misunderstood?" She could feel her heart rate kick up a notch or two. He *was* interested. "I'm absolutely free tomorrow. And I'd love to have a native show me around the city. Where shall I meet you and what time?"

"Let's start with Pike Place Market. About two. Wear warm clothes. We might do something near the water. And if you're up for it, we can have dinner in an Italian place I know nearby."

"Are you sure you want to spend all day playing guide?"

He grinned. "Oh, I'm willing to throw myself on this particular grenade. For the good of the city, of course."

"Right. The good of the city." She grinned back. "Okay, then, the Market, dinner, and whatever else you have in mind sounds great."

"I'll make reservations at the restaurant, assuming they have a table available. They're busy on Saturdays because they have interesting entertainment as well as good food."

By the time they had firmed up their plans for the next day, they were on the way out of the bistro. "Thank you for dinner. It was fun," she said.

"You're welcome. I enjoyed it, too. Do you have a car around someplace?" he asked.

"In the garage near your building."

"I'll walk you there."

From the look in his eyes when they reached her little Kia, she thought he might be about to kiss her. Instead, he merely touched her face with the tips of his fingers and said, "See you tomorrow, then."

Every cell in her cheek woke up and told its neighbor to pay attention to what was going on. The awareness of his touch went down her face to her neck and chest and would have traveled even further if he hadn't moved his hand.

It took a deep gulp of oxygen to unscramble her brain so she could pay attention to what was going on. His mouth was doing something. Not kissing her, sadly, but maybe saying something. At least she thought he was talking about something. It was difficult to tell when she was this discombobulated.

"Do you know where it is?" he was asking when she tuned back in to him.

Unfortunately, she had no idea what he was talking about. "Where *what* is?"

"The place in the Market where the guys throw the fish around."

She hoped it was too dark for him to see how fast she was turning red from embarrassment but managed to get out, "I think I do. It's at the main entrance, isn't it?"

"Exactly. Meet me there at two."

Chapter Eleven

Excited about the day ahead of her, Bella got to the Pike Place Market well before two. While she waited for Taylor, she watched the two men behind the seafood counter put on a show for their customers, as well as anyone else who cared to watch, with an entertaining line of patter and fish tossing. She was so engrossed, she didn't realize Taylor was standing behind her until she heard him say close to her ear, "Fun to see, aren't they?"

Not nearly as fun as feeling his warm breath on her neck, she decided, but it wasn't a good idea to jump right to such an intimate comment, so she merely laughed and nodded. "After I watched for a while, I wondered if the job interview for fishmonger here includes a test to see how proficient you are at throwing and catching seafood," she said.

"I've never thought to ask, but I imagine the answer's yes." He held out his hand to her. "If you've had your fill of salmon tossing, we're burning daylight here and we have a lot of things to see before dinner."

There it was again, the tingle from contact with his hand. But she barely had time to enjoy it before he was tugging at her to come with him. So she held on to his hand and followed, taking much bigger steps than normal to keep up with his long legs. He was obviously serious about showing her around, and she intended to enjoy every minute of it.

After a couple hours, however, she said, "I surrender. There is way too much here for me to take in on one visit. The craft choices alone are overwhelming. I have to remember those handmade puzzles when the holidays roll around. My nieces and nephews would love them. And my father would have told the glass artist we saw he belongs in the Museum of Glass, not a farmers' market."

"If you know about the Museum of Glass, you're not the new arrival in the area you pretended to be yesterday, are you?" His raised eyebrow and half smile said he wasn't too worried about being hoodwinked.

"Nate asked what I'd done in Seattle since I moved here, and I told him. I wasn't asked if I'd been here before. But, no, I'm not a complete newbie. Two or three years ago, I came up to a baseball game. On another trip, I went to the Museum of Glass in Tacoma and the Chihuly Garden and Glass museum here. Both trips were with my father."

"He hasn't brought you back since?"

"He died eighteen months ago." She turned her head so he wouldn't see her fight to control the tears that were unexpectedly welling up in her eyes. "We took a lot of road trips the last year or so of his life. There were things he wanted to see one last time before he died, and I made it happen for him."

Taylor stopped and brushed away an escaping tear with the pad of his thumb. "I didn't mean to bring up a sad subject."

"No, it's fine. I don't know why I'm reacting this way. It's been a long time since I cried about his passing." She pulled a tissue from her purse and wiped at her eyes. "We had a lot of fun that last year. Drove all over the Northwest. Well, the part west of the mountains. He was never much of a high plains guy." Another tissue was necessary for her nose. "I don't know. Maybe it was seeing the beautiful glass. He was a serious collector of studio art glass and was always sure one day he'd discover the next Dale Chihuly or Silvia Levenson. He never did but he kept trying. The closest he got was buying a piece of Amanda Sinclair's before she got too pricey."

"I know who Chihuly is. Who're the two women?"

"Levenson does glass casting mostly. Pale pink glass hand grenades. High heel shoes with barbed wire inclusions. Sinclair is a Portlander who does mostly minimalist landscapes in thick blocks. Lately she's been using a lot of metals and reactive glasses."

"Sounds like you know something about the subject yourself."

"It was hard not to learn about it. I lived with my dad for the last years of his life and helped him take care of his collection." She shoved the tissues into her jeans pocket. "There. Trip down memory lane is over. Sorry to be Debbie Downer. I promise I won't do it again. Maybe my caffeine level had dropped too low. How about we grab a quick cup of coffee before we move on to whatever else you have planned?"

"Not a problem. There's a bakery back that way, across the street ..."

She glanced at the storefront he indicated. "Oh, I saw some beautiful little hand pies in the window when we walked past. It looks perfect. But first, can we go back to the pig sculpture? I forgot to rub her snout for good luck."

"What do you need good luck for?"

"Not for me. It's for Summer's project. We need all the luck we can get."

She saw his jaw muscles clench and his lips thin. He looked like he did yesterday when he'd found her in Nate's office. Something had made him tense up. "Is there a problem with backtracking?" she asked, hoping it wasn't what she'd suggested.

Without answering her question, he reached for her hand again and headed for the sculpture. When they got there, she noticed he didn't participate in the ritual of touching the nose and making a small donation. She couldn't decide if he was anti-superstition, annoyed she'd upset his plans, or something else. Something she couldn't figure out.

As they headed back to the bakery, she said, "Thank you for indulging me. The pig thing is silly, I know. But ..."

"It's part of the Market's culture, and I'm glad you reminded me about it. Now let's get you some caffeine and sugar so you're stoked up for what's next."

And there he was; the Taylor she enjoyed was back. He'd turned his attitude around on a dime, and she couldn't figure out how or why any more than she could figure out what had made it tense only a few minutes before. All she could do was go with it. So she asked, "What *is* next, by the way? Or are you going to keep me in suspense until we get there?"

• • •

Taylor got her settled at a small table in the bakery before he went to order their coffee. Now that he had his back to her and she couldn't see his face, he let his guard down and frowned. He should never have started this. Never gone into the bar last night. Never asked her out for today. Didn't his immediate guilty reaction to her request to go back to the pig sculpture to wish for luck for her project prove he was wrong to have anything to do with her?

He should never ... oh, hell, what was the use? He'd been attracted to her from the first minute he saw her, and this was the logical outcome. He either had to accept that he was metal filings to her magnet—which sounded faintly dirty, come to think of it—or else find a way to turn her into something to repel him.

Which, so far, had been impossible. He snuck a peek at her. She was sitting at the table playing with her smart phone, checking e-mails, probably. How could anyone so beautiful repel any man in his right mind?

He couldn't remember the last time he noticed in any detail what a woman wore, but he seemed to always be aware of what Isabella had on. Maybe it was because she knew how to wear clothes to showcase her considerable assets.

Today her jeans outlined her butt and legs; her bunny-soft, sky-blue sweater hugged the curves her jeans didn't cover. A dark red puffy jacket made her look tiny and delicate until you saw the kick-ass boots she wore that came halfway up her legs and had heels high enough to make him wonder how she had ever kept up with him as he strode through the crowds in the Market. She even smelled good, like a sugar cookie. Vanilla, maybe.

It was time to man up, admit he was in trouble with her and enjoy it. Instead of thinking of all the reasons he should get the hell out of here and head for home, he should be thanking his luck he was having the best Saturday he'd had in months.

With a woman who was kick-ass, sexy, sweet, and funny. A woman who delighted in what she saw around her and allowed herself to show vulnerability in a way he couldn't begin to comprehend. He never talked about his family in any but the most general terms. Never let anyone know what his childhood had been like or how estranged from his family he'd become as an adult. He told himself it was because he didn't want anyone's pity. But it didn't take a shrink to figure out it was really because it was too painful to think about, let alone discuss with someone else.

Isabella, on the other hand, had just revealed her heart to a virtual stranger when she talked about her father. What would it be like to be the object of the affection and attention of a woman like her? Someone so present, so open, so warm and loving?

Oh, yeah. He was in a world of hurt with Isabella Rodriquez.

• • •

"Thanks for the coffee and treat. I'm ready now." She swiped at her mouth with the napkin but missed a pastry crumb. He almost reached across the table to brush it off her lip. Her plump, pink, lower lip. The one she was now licking to get at the errant crumb. The same one she caught between her teeth when she was trying not to laugh or when she was thinking about what she wanted to say.

"Taylor? Are we ready for whatever's next?" She looked concerned when he hadn't responded right away, too caught up in fantasies about her mouth.

"Absolutely ready. We're going for a ride." He picked up their coffee cups and the plates now empty of the apple hand pies they'd had and returned them to the counter.

"My car or yours?" she asked when he returned.

"Neither. We're walking down the steps behind the Market then along the waterfront to the ferry terminal. It's not too far, about fifteen or twenty minutes. You okay with walking? I don't want you to end up with blisters from those boots."

"Are you kidding? I was born to walk in boots like this." She looked back over her shoulder as they headed to the door and asked, "What're we going to do when we get to the ferry terminal? As if I can't guess."

"Unless you want to confine yourself to reading the timetables for the Washington State Ferry System, I thought we could take a ride. We'll be 'walk-ons' for the next ferry to Bainbridge Island. I think you'll like seeing the city from the water."

"I don't know where Bainbridge Island is."

"It's about forty-five minutes west of here, across Elliot Bay. We'll get there, have another cup of coffee, or a glass of wine if you'd rather, then come back. Should get us here in plenty of time for our dinner reservations."

• • •

They lucked out and got to the ferry terminal twenty minutes before a Bainbridge Island ferry was due to depart. They boarded and grabbed a seat near a window, but Isabella didn't stay in it very long. Her curiosity sent her exploring all over the passenger deck. She returned from one foray with a stack of tourist pamphlets, which she excitedly showed him, explaining they gave her ideas for the weekends she didn't have a tour guide. He stopped himself just before he volunteered as a permanent tour guide. He'd waded into hip-deep treacherous waters already with this woman. Planning too far out with her would get him in over his head.

As soon as the ferry got underway, Isabella headed for the door and the outside rail. She was as excited as anyone he'd ever seen about watching the skyline of Seattle recede into the distance.

"Look at all those buildings," she said. "When I'm in the middle of the city, it doesn't register how tall they are."

"I think it's the hills the city is built on. You can't get an idea of the relative heights until you're out on the water."

"What's that one, over there?" she asked, pointing to a huge, black building.

"The Columbia Center. It's the tallest building in the state. Sometimes when the weather socks in during the winter, the top of the building is above the clouds. It's freaky."

"What else can we see?"

"Couple of bank buildings—Wells Fargo and Bank of America." He pointed out the relevant structures. "There's the Federal Building named for our late, great Senator 'Scoop' Jackson. Then there's that one," he said, pointing to Seattle's most famous landmark. "I assume you know ..."

"The Space Needle. Of course I do. And I know another one, too. Isn't that Smith Tower?" She pointed at the correct building.

"Yes, but don't look so smug. I'm pretty sure you're required to identify those two buildings along with Safeco Field on the test they give you before you're allowed to move into the city."

She looked at him with a surprised expression. "Why, Taylor Jordan, you have a sense of humor under all those wicked smarts and serious ambitions, don't you?"

He could feel himself blush, for the second time in two days. How did she do this to him? "I try to keep it to a minimum, but sometimes it leaks out."

She laughed. "You are the sweetest man." He saw her shudder.

"I can't imagine my ranking on a sugar scale is what's making you shiver. You must be cold."

"I am, a little. The wind, I guess. I thought this coat would keep me warm but, so far, not so much."

"Then let's go back inside."

"No, I'm not ready yet. I like it out here too much regardless of the temperature." She pulled the collar of her puffy coat up around her ears and faced the water again. "I mean, how can I go inside when I'll miss all this if I do?" The sweep of her hand took in the skyline of the city, the water of Elliot Bay, and the gulls and terns flying overhead.

Knowing what he was about to do pushed him further out into bottomless waters, but wanting to do it anyway, Taylor opened his coat and wrapped it around her, pulling her so her back was snug against his front. "Maybe this will help," he said. He felt her relax against him and sigh.

"Thank you. That's wonderful. You're like a heater, aren't you?"

He rested his cheek on the top of her head, smelled the flowery scent of her shampoo, the sugar cookie smell of her perfume or, who knows, maybe her body. She might think he was sweet, but he was sure he didn't smell like she did.

She slid her hands under his, to get them warm, maybe. Whatever the reason, he was glad she was doing it. Her hands felt so small in his, so delicate.

So cold.

"Are you sure you don't want to go inside? Your hands are like ice."

"A few more minutes, please? I love it out here."

So did he. And with much more of this, she'd see exactly how much he loved having her plastered against his body, regardless of how cold it was. He tried to move so his beginning arousal wasn't quite so obvious.

"Are you cold, too?" she asked. "I didn't ask if you wanted to go inside."

"I'm fine. But I don't want you to get so frozen you won't defrost before we have to get back on the ferry and do this all over again."

She turned in his arms and looked up at him. "I could never get too cold with you around."

He pulled her closer, knowing what he was about to do had been inevitable since the first time he saw her. He was going to kiss her, and he already knew he was going to love every single second of it.

Tilting his head so he had the angle he wanted, he brushed her mouth with his. He felt her breath against his lips and the need to taste her welled up in him. Her mouth was warm and soft, as luscious as he'd imagined it would be. Before he even asked with his tongue, her lips parted, allowing him to explore her mouth as she sighed, her breath becoming the air filling his lungs.

He sucked at the plump center of her lower lip, and she moaned. The shivers he felt race through her weren't from cold this time, he was sure. When he broke the kiss, her whimper of disappointment stoked his arousal and he had to fight his urge to press his hips against her.

With light, careful kisses, he traced a path from the corner of her mouth to her cheek and jaw to the soft place behind her ear where he nibbled. But she apparently wanted something else. She took his face in her hands and returned his mouth to hers for another long, hot, open-mouthed kiss with tangling tongues and a soundtrack of her moans and sighs.

It wasn't until someone said, "Get a room, you two," that Taylor came to his senses and broke from the kiss.

"I'm sorry. I got carried away," he said, looking directly at her to see how she was reacting.

"Nothing to apologize for, believe me. I'm about as warm now as I can bear." He was relieved to see she was amused and maybe a bit aroused. "But I do think we should go back inside, don't you? We've been the entertainment for long enough."

Chapter Twelve

It could have been awkward between them after the scene outside. Bella was worried it would be. But it wasn't. The occasional tension that appeared between them when they were together seemed to have relaxed with their outdoor make-out session. And since she'd wanted him to kiss her the minute she saw him at Pike Place Market, even having him apologize for doing what she'd hoped for didn't dent her pleasure.

Disembarking from the ferry, they wandered around Bainbridge Island for an hour, peeking into art galleries and small shops and sipping wine in a cozy bar, before reboarding the ferry for the trip back to the city. This time, they stayed inside the whole way. She even dozed off for a few minutes, her head resting on Taylor's shoulder.

He teased her when he had to wake her as the ferry docked. "I had no idea I could wear you out so quickly."

"It's the sea air," she said struggling to sit up and smooth out her hair. "It always makes me sleepy."

"Maybe a break would be a good idea before we go to dinner. What do you think?"

"I would appreciate a chance to see if I can do something to get my hair to behave." She tugged at a handful of windblown curls, which had gotten kinkier and tighter in the damp air.

He pulled her hand away. "Don't do anything drastic with your curls. I like them the way they are."

"I never do anything drastic. It's too time consuming to keep it ironed or conditioned or straightened. But I do like it out of my face, and right now that requires a mirror and a couple clips."

"If you have the clips, I can provide you with a mirror. My condo isn't too far away from here if that would be acceptable to you. I can warm you up, too." Before she could ask exactly how he planned to do that, he added, "Your friend Marius taught me how to make good coffee. Our dinner reservation isn't until seven."

"Perfect. But I have to retrieve my car. Do you want to give me directions, or shall I follow you?"

"I walked to the Market. You can give me a ride."

•••

She wasn't sure what she expected Taylor's condo to look like. But when he opened the door, she realized how right the space looked. Neat, carefully planned, and organized. A chocolate-brown leather couch. Side chairs covered in a beige linen-like fabric. Hardwood floors with not a nick, dent, or scratch in sight. The only bright colors were in the design of the oval rug in front of the couch and in the large abstract painting above the obligatory gas fireplace.

She was quite sure that if someone came into her place without warning, there would be newspapers or books flung on tables and chairs, perhaps an empty coffee mug on a kitchen counter, maybe even dirty dishes in the sink. Not in Taylor's home. Everything was in its place. Of course, he could have planned in advance to invite her in, but she was willing to bet his home looked this tidy all the time.

"Your condo is beautiful. Have you lived here long?"

"About six months. But it's not much bigger than the place I had rented before, so things came together easily. I'm glad you like it." He led her to a small but well-appointed kitchen. "Coffee or wine? Or I could probably dig up a beer or a can of pop if you'd rather."

"Something hot, I think. So, coffee, thanks." While he was grinding beans and getting the coffeemaker set up to brew, she went into the bathroom to try to tame her wayward hair. After success of a sort—it was at least not tangled and hanging in her face—she wandered into the small dining area off the kitchen, looking at a display of pictures on the sideboard. She was surprised to see all except one were landscapes. "Is this your family?" she asked, picking up the one photograph of people.

"Yeah, I'm the skinny little one on the right."

"So, you're the younger?"

"By five years." He handed her a mug of coffee. "Sugar or milk?"

"No, this is fine, thanks."

Before she could ask any more about his family, he changed the subject. "Do you have siblings?"

She snorted. "Boy, do I. Four brothers. All older."

"And I bet all very protective of their baby sister."

"I might as well have been in a convent in high school. Didn't date much until I went to college, and even then, they demanded background information on everyone I so much as thought about going out with."

"How'd you handle that?"

"I learned to be creative. Either I omitted telling them what I was doing, or I embroidered it so they were comfortable. To this day, they think the guy I dated the longest in college was headed for the priesthood. Which would have been interesting since he was Jewish."

Taylor laughed. "Are any of your brothers around here, and do they still track down your dates and cross-examine them? I'm getting a little worried here about who might call on me in the next day or two."

"No worries. They all live in California. They do call me every week to make sure I've not been kidnapped. And Javier, the youngest, sometimes shows up in Seattle. He's done business here in the past. I think he dated Sandra Daniels for a while, actually."

"Is he bigger than me?"

She pretended to consider the question. "I think he might be a couple inches shorter. But he could be younger than you are. He's only eighteen months older than I am, which makes him almost twenty-nine."

"Damn. He *is* younger."

"But it shouldn't be a problem, should it? We're not dating, remember? You don't date clients."

"Saved by unofficial company policy." He gestured to her to follow him into the living room. When they were settled on the couch, he said, "Tell me more about your family. I've always wondered what it would be like to grow up in a big family."

So Bella regaled him with stories of her childhood, hitting the highlights and relating only good memories. It surprised her to realize how much of the anger she'd felt about her brothers forcing her to move out of the house in Portland had faded. In fact, the longer she talked, the more she realized that although she hadn't gotten to grateful yet, she was pleased to discover she was past furious.

She was also surprised Taylor didn't reciprocate. No matter how subtly she made inquiries, he didn't respond with any information about his family.

• • •

As he listened to her talk about her siblings with such warmth, it occurred to Taylor he should have planned the day better. He'd left too much time for talking. Which presented too much temptation to spill his guts, which he never, ever did. She made it seem so easy to talk about family. Even when she was complaining about them, it was with love. And she made it perfectly obvious she wanted him to talk about his background. After all, isn't that basic getting-to-know-you conversation?

But how the hell do you talk about the miserable excuse for parents and a sibling he had right after she babbled on about her storybook childhood? In what fairy tale is your brother a drunk starting in high school? Your father so irresponsible and careless with money, they lived in a McMansion one year and the back of a secondhand SUV the next? How did he explain how guilty he felt he hadn't been able to rescue his beaten down, pale ghost of a mother who had slipped quietly out of life in her forties, too tired of the vagaries of life with his father to keep breathing?

He hadn't seen his brother in a decade or so, didn't know where he was but was pretty sure it was in the bottom of a bottle someplace. He knew where his father was—in the small house Taylor had bought for him in Spokane. Far enough away that he didn't have to see him often but close enough if he needed to get to him. He hadn't needed to in quite some time.

No, talking about his pathetic excuse for a family, after she'd talked so glowingly about hers, would only make her pity him. Although he hadn't yet decided what he wanted her to feel for him, he knew without a doubt, it wasn't pity.

He wished he hadn't left the damn picture on the sideboard. He'd put it away as soon as he got home from dinner.

• • •

Something had made Taylor grow quiet, and once again, Bella couldn't figure out what it was. She didn't think she'd said or done anything stupid, although given how little she knew about him, it was always possible. She didn't feel confident enough to ask him directly so she merely said, "You're the one who seems tired now. Do you want to skip dinner? We've had a full day and I ..."

"Absolutely not. I've been looking forward to showing you this place all day. It's practically a Seattle institution." He glanced at the clock on the bookcase shelf. "And we're about due there, if you're ready." He took their coffee mugs into the kitchen and retrieved her puffy coat from the coat rack in the hall. "We're walking, if that's okay with you."

The Pink Door was as Taylor had advertised. The food was amazing. Bella ordered risotto with crab, saffron, and leeks. Taylor didn't even look at the menu. He said he always had the lasagna because it was so good he couldn't bring himself to try anything else. As the entertainment for the evening began, they shared an antipasto plate and wine.

First up was a troop of gymnasts above them on silk drapes and huge hoops, twirling, twisting, and dropping to the ground with grace. By the time their entrees arrived, the scene had changed. A pair of musicians played while a man sang opera arias.

The walk back to her car after dinner was slow and, on her part, reluctant. "I've had the most wonderful day. I can't even begin to thank you enough."

"You paid for dinner behind my back, which was a pretty big thank you already."

"You paid for everything else today and provided guide services. I had to do something for what I owed you."

"No, I owe you for today." They were standing beside her car, and he'd turned her toward him, his hands on her shoulders. "And I always pay my debts."

She started to ask what he could possibly owe her, but then she looked into his eyes. The summer blue-sky color she'd seen there all day was now dark and hot. Hotter than any summer sky she'd ever known.

Her breath caught in her throat as his hands moved up from her shoulders, caressing her neck on their way to cupping her face. He was going to kiss her again. She knew it. She wanted it. She licked her lips in anticipation.

But instead of kissing her, he said, "I don't know how you do it, but you make me feel more alive than anyone I've ever met. Today, seeing the city, the water, even the fish tossing, through your eyes was amazing. You were the guide today. The guide to being happy and content with life. That's what I owe you."

She circled his neck with her arms and took a step closer to him. "And how do you propose to pay your debt, Mr. Jordan?"

He showed her by pressing her against her car then moving his hands to her hips and pulling her close so she could feel exactly how he might pay off what he said he owed her. Slanting her head to meet his mouth in the right place, he brushed his lips against hers then used the tip of his tongue to explore from one corner of her mouth to the other. He teased her mouth open, stroked her tongue, asking her to join him in the dance.

She tasted the wine they'd had for dinner, heard the groan from the back of his throat as his tongue made love to her mouth, smelled the citrus aftershave he wore, felt the warmth of his hands on her body.

The kiss was even steamier than the one on the ferry. His hands roamed up and over her hips to her waist and then the sides of her breasts. She knew any second he would discover how tight and hard her nipples were, wanted him to find out what his kiss did to her.

Instead, he drew back, touched her forehead with his, moved his hands down to her waist. "This isn't the time or the place for this, is it?"

"Probably not," she agreed. "But it was nice."

He smiled. "Nice? Yes, it was nice." He gave her one more kiss on the forehead before stepping back. "We'll have to do this again, won't we?"

"Yes, I'd like to." She opened the driver's side door and slid in.

"Will you text me to let me know you got home okay?"

"I don't have your phone number."

"Give me your cellphone, please." When she retrieved it from the bottom of her purse, he punched in his number. "Now you do."

• • •

"You're in a remarkably good mood for a Monday morning," Nate said as he passed Taylor in the hall. "You're humming. I've never heard you hum before. It must have been a hell of a weekend." He stopped and waited for an explanation.

"On my way to work this morning, I heard a song I liked coming from someone's car. Must have gotten it stuck in my head." Taylor wasn't sure he was ready to share his weekend with anyone, much less the architect of the fix-up on Friday, so he tried to walk on by.

Nate was not about to let the conversation end, however. "Right. It's an earworm." If he ever snorted, it would have been right then. "You can't fool me. I have a feeling my sneaky plan yielded good results for one cute little brunette and you."

When Taylor didn't turn around or respond, Nate said, "Come on. Humor me. I'm stuck in the middle of a divorce, which has been dragging on forever, and have to live my life through other people. I'd like to know *someone* is having a decent, normal social life. Won't you at least answer one question—did you or did you not take Bella Rodriguez on a tour of the city?"

Taylor stood still for a moment before his good mood softened his resolve to keep his extraordinary weekend all to himself. "I met her downstairs for a drink on Friday after work. And then we went to dinner."

He ran his fingers over his jawline, trying to decide if he had fed Nate's curiosity enough and if he wanted to admit to the rest. "You get enough jollies, or do you want more?"

"Is there more? If there is, then hell, yes, I want it."

Damn. He'd have to remember to watch his words more carefully. "We went to the Market on Saturday, then took a ferry ride."

"How romantic of you. I didn't think you had it in you." Nate wrinkled his brow. "But that's not all, is it?"

"We had dinner again." Taylor finally turned and glared at his friend. "*Now* can I get to work, please?"

"I'm impressed. And happy for you both. You need to get back into circulation, and she needs a friend in town. Not to mention some diversion from the problems they're having getting Summer's business up and running. Did she talk about it at all?"

"No, we pretty much stayed away from talking about work." Because if she ever found out he'd had a hand in creating her problems, she'd be so pissed she'd never speak to him again. "I better get to work before I forget what I'm supposed to be doing." Or give in to the temptation to confess what he'd done and see if there was any way out so he could keep seeing her.

• • •

"Morning, girlfriend. What's up for your week?" Summer began their Monday morning Skype session with the usual question.

"I went over the marketing plan with Nate last Friday so I have all my notes to organize and get to you. Then I thought I'd ..."

"Wait. Rewind. You went over it *with* him. You didn't send it to him?"

Bella realized what she'd gotten herself into and now needed to get out of. "Well, yes. I thought it would be better if we talked it over in person instead of through e-mails. You know how impersonal and imprecise e-mailing can be."

"Yes, I also know how eager you were for the Viking god to call you. So I'm guessing he didn't and you decided to force his hand. Nice work. Can we do a virtual high-five, girlfriend?"

"You don't mind that you'll get billed for the forty-five minutes Nate and I talked so I could see Taylor Jordan?"

"If I say it's a good investment in the mental health of my employee, will you tell me if it paid off?"

Bella sank back in her chair, grinning. "We had drinks and dinner on Friday. Then on Saturday, he played tour guide a bit and showed me some of Seattle before we had dinner again. It was a great day."

"So ...?"

She waited for Summer to say more. She didn't. "Is there a question there?" she finally asked.

"You do realize I can see you, don't you? And what I see is the look of a woman who's quite happy with herself. Let me repeat, and with even more emphasis, *so* ...?"

"There's no more to tell. We had a great time. He kissed me goodbye after dinner and said we'd do it again—I think he meant the sightseeing but he could have meant the kiss—but we didn't make definite plans." She leaned forward onto her forearms. "He's interesting, if a little strange about some things. Probably the most organized person I've ever met. You should see his condo ..."

"Whoa, whoa. Not so fast. You were in his condo? That bit of information didn't make it into the description of what you'd done on Saturday. Or did you stay Saturday night and were there Sunday morning, too?"

"Oh, for heaven's sake, Summer. You know me better. I don't fall into bed with just anyone. We went there between the ferry ride and dinner to defrost with a cup of coffee. What I started to say was, it's so neat, it's like it's been staged by a real estate broker. Everything in place. And he's only been there a few months, he said. It takes me a year to get settled, and even then I move things around every few months forever."

"You don't mean he's OCD organized, do you?"

"No, he's not extreme. He's, well, organized in an ordinary way, I'd say. He says he plans everything carefully. I get the impression he likes to be in control."

"Not dangerously in need of controlling things, I hope."

"He didn't try to force me to do anything or get upset when I veered from what he had planned for the day, if that's what you mean."

"Because I don't think you need any more males in your life telling you what to do."

"I absolutely agree. It's not his need for organizing things I thought was strange. It was not talking very much about himself. He was more interested in listening to me talk about my family than in talking about his."

"A man who wants to listen to you talk about yourself? Good God, girl, grab him. His kind is practically extinct."

"Maybe. But there's something, I don't know, different about him. He blows hot and cold really fast. One minute, we're holding hands, and the next minute, he's totally off someplace where I'm not. It confuses me. Mostly, I guess, because I can't figure out what sets it off."

"So if he confuses you, what makes him so interesting to you?"

"When he's totally there, completely with me, he's amazing. Funny, smart, sweet. I've never met anyone quite like him."

"And I infer from earlier conversations you think sexy is in the mix."

"Duh. Viking god who kisses like an angel."

"Guess that means you're going to have to see him again so you can try to figure him out."

She laughed. "I guess so."

"Good. That's settled. Now about the marketing plan."

Chapter Thirteen

It didn't take long to get the marketing plan sorted out. And when it was, Bella started on her assignment—developing the information they needed for a company brochure. She began to mine the computer files to locate the names and contact information for former BU/MU clients in the Seattle area. She would be reaching out to them to see if they'd be willing to be quoted on their experience with BU/MU's services. Even if it was only reviewing computer files, it was exciting to have something else to do other than try to budge the immovable City of Seattle into granting a zoning change.

But when she made her weekly call to the planning department to see if any progress had been made, she got unexpected good news. The hearing for their application had finally been scheduled. It would take place on Wednesday afternoon of the following week. And the city staffer told her, he was reasonably confident the only opposition would be Mrs. Pennington, the neighborhood association president. The planning commission would respectfully listen and then make a decision based on the staff recommendation, which he thought she would "find acceptable" to use his words. He didn't say it was a done deal, but his comment was close enough to make her feel confident she had good news to report to Summer.

Between researching files and prepping for the hearing, she almost forgot about Taylor's somewhat-less-than-a-promise to see her again. Almost. She dreamed about his kisses a couple times, dreams from which she woke up aroused and crabby to find it hadn't been real. But there was nothing more she was willing to do to get the next kiss. She had no more excuses to go to the MBA offices, and since she had made the first move the last time, it was his turn.

He made it on Thursday with a welcome phone call.

"Nate tells me you got some good news from the city," he said.

"We did. The staffer responsible for our application said it looked pretty good because no one else had come out of the woodwork to oppose us. I have my fingers crossed and a construction team on standby to start the renovations we need the day after the vote."

"Congratulations. Persistence must be your middle name."

"It's a quality I had to dig deep for, but it's coming in handy for all sorts of things right now." As soon as she made the comment, she realized it could be taken to mean more than just in dealing with the city. She was appalled at herself and hoped he wouldn't pick up on it.

He didn't seem to. "I'm happy for you. And Summer, of course. But the reason I called was to ask if you have anything planned for Sunday. I thought we might have brunch and then go to the Olympic Sculpture Garden. The weather's supposed to be decent enough to be outside."

"It sounds terrific. I'd love to. What time and where shall I meet you?"

"I'll come pick you up this time. About ten?"

"Perfect."

It took her a few minutes after they ended the phone call to get back her focus on work. She spent that much time wondering how long after he picked her up it would take for him to find an excuse to kiss her. She hoped it was immediately, if not sooner.

• • •

Taylor had deliberately not told her he was taking her to brunch at the Space Needle restaurant, wanting to make the beginning of their day together a surprise. He got the reaction he wanted as they drove in the direction of the Seattle landmark.

"We're going to the Space Needle?" she asked. Well, yelled actually, then clapped her hands, before grapping his arm and hugging it. "I can't believe it! Didn't you say it was too touristy?"

"I did and it is. But the food isn't bad, the view is spectacular, and you haven't been there. So, here we are." He parked the car and came around to open her door.

"Thank you for this. It's really so sweet of you."

"There you go again. If you keep saying I'm sweet, I might begin to believe it and lose my killer edge."

She twined her arm through his as they walked from the car, and she didn't let go while they rode up in the elevator. Her grin was infectious, apparently, because everyone in the elevator who looked at her smiled, too. Even he had to fight to keep his lips from curling up into something resembling the expression of sheer pleasure she had on her face.

He was glad she was holding on to him while they were being led to their table. Captivated by the view, Isabella wasn't paying much attention to where she was walking, and twice Taylor had to catch her as she stumbled.

Once seated, he ordered champagne for them to enjoy as they perused the menu. When their server returned with their wine, they ordered: eggs Benedict with Dungeness crab for her, a garden scramble for him. She teased him about being so health conscious when they were doing something so out of the ordinary. He threatened to compare their cholesterol levels when brunch was over.

As they waited for their entrees, he watched her look out the window at the ever-changing scenery as the restaurant slowly circled around the center core of the structure. He'd never been with anyone who was so present, so open to enjoyment, so happy to be where she was. It was a revelation to him. Instead of only looking ahead, she soaked in what was around her, brought joy and passion to the moment.

He couldn't help wondering if she brought the same joy and passion into bed with her. Not that he was going to take her to bed. Sex with her would be a bad idea. The sex would be good, he was sure. The aftermath would be tough to deal with.

But he still wondered, if he did, if he could, what would it be like? How would she sound when she came? He knew how responsive she was to his kisses. Would she be just as responsive to caresses on other parts of her body?

He could feel most his of blood leave his brain for southern latitudes as he pictured a naked and needy Isabella in his bed. It was about as inappropriate a response to brunch at the Space Needle restaurant as he could imagine. He had to get himself under control, or he'd do something really stupid, something to further complicate an already complex situation.

Except when he was with her, nothing seemed difficult or complicated. It was all straightforward. He was with a beautiful woman who seemed to find pleasure in everything she did. Who made him feel happy to merely sit across a table from her and watch her enjoy the view outside the window. A beautiful woman he wanted to take to his bed and keep her there until he figured out the secret.

• • •

Now where is he? she wondered. He was doing one of those retreat things he seemed to do fairly regularly with her. If only she knew what he was thinking.

Oh, what the hell. She had nothing to lose, did she? The worst he could do was refuse to answer. So she took the chance and asked, "Taylor, where do you go when you glaze over and disappear?"

He quite literally shook himself to come back to the conversation. "I'm sorry. Was I being rude? I was thinking. Just thinking. That's all."

"What about? Or is it so secret that if you told me, you'd have to throw me off the observation platform?"

"I can't think of anything I know to warrant such an extreme action."

"Then what?"

She watched several expressions race across his face. Fear, oddly enough, was the first one. Then a thoughtful look, followed by a more determined one. "The truth is, I was wondering how to steal something from you."

"What in the world do I have that you want?"

"It's your ability to, I don't know, get pleasure out of everything you do. It's like you have pixie dust you sprinkle all over where you are to make you happy."

"On a list of all the things I could have guessed, pixie dust wouldn't have made the first hundred. Maybe even the first thousand."

"It sounds silly, I know. But I don't know how else to explain it. You have this almost magic ability to be in the present in a way that eludes me. Or at least is buried so deep inside me I can't find it."

She could feel hope begin to blossom in her. He was finally opening up about something personal. "Why do you think you aren't in the present? I mean, sometimes it seems your mind wanders, and I know you have a lot of responsibility at work. But you're here with me now. And have been most of the time we've spent together."

"It's more than a wandering mind, I'm afraid, although I'm relieved you don't feel neglected. I thought I might have made you uncomfortable a couple times."

She was surprised he was so aware of her reaction to him. "Not uncomfortable. Curious. Like I said, I wondered where you went when you got that look on your face."

"Sometimes I'm afraid I've forgotten, if I ever knew, how to enjoy where I am and whom I'm with. I've spent most of my life looking ahead, planning the next step. You make me want to know your secret for enjoying the moment without losing it in anticipating what's next."

She laughed. "I wish my brothers could hear you. They think the way I do things is the wrong way. They say I've spent all my adult life purposely *avoiding* looking ahead."

"That's not true, is it?"

"Like a lot of things, there's an element of truth in it. I haven't planned my life out, not the way you describe you have. I've always done what my family wanted me to do, been the perfect daughter. What I wanted to do myself sort of fell by the wayside at some point."

"What was it you wanted to do?"

"Write. But it's hard to support yourself with writing fiction until you have a name and a few books under your belt. I ended up running the family's real estate office in California until I moved to Portland to take care of ailing parents."

"How'd you connect with Summer?"

"At a luncheon. We clicked, and she hired me to ghost letters for her clients."

Immediately, an expression of fear took over from the other expressions on Taylor's face.

• • •

Shit. Not only does she work for Summer but she writes the damn letters. Suppose she was the one who wrote Allison's letter? No, fate wouldn't be that cruel. He had to end this conversation right now.

Luckily, their food arrived, and the need to change subjects was buried in their appreciation of the excellent meals. Topping it off with coffee and a shared cobbler, the subject of her work with BU/MU didn't come up again. Thank God.

It didn't surface as they wandered through the Olympic Sculpture Garden either. One of Taylor's favorite places in the city, he led Isabella to the pieces he loved the most—the pair of giant eyes, the huge abstract design by Louise Bourgeois, the ampersand, all set against the backdrop of the Puget Sound. It was a perfect day. No rain, a bit of sun peeking through the clouds and reflecting off the water. It was chilly but not cold enough to want to be inside. Which was a good thing. The PACCAR Pavilion, where more of the art was exhibited, was closed to the public because a wedding was taking place there.

Usually being with a woman anywhere near a wedding made Taylor skittish. Too much chance an inappropriate woman would get ideas he didn't want her to have. But this time, he wasn't nervous. Isabella commented on what a lovely venue it was for a wedding ceremony, he agreed, and they went back to looking at massive sculptures. No further discussion. No uncomfortable silences. No meaningful glances at left hands and ring fingers.

He didn't stop to think why having her comment on a wedding didn't bother him. Any more than he stopped to think why he'd always been drawn to the sculpture called "Father and Son."

As they walked away from the building, a buzz came from his phone. "Sorry, I have to take this," he said when he saw who was calling.

"Not a problem. I'll be over by the ampersand when you're finished. I didn't get a photo of it."

A couple minutes later, he joined her. "As much as I hate to end this, I have to get you home. My evening mentoring session got moved up to an hour from now."

"Mentoring? With whom?" she asked, then quickly added, "You don't have to tell me, of course. It's really none of my business."

"There's no reason not to tell you. I mentor the owners of a couple small—as in, one person—businesses."

"I didn't know MBA worked with such small companies. I'm impressed."

"We don't. I'm part of a volunteer, nonprofit program that does."

"Aren't you competing with your own firm?"

He laughed. "None of the businesses I've ever worked with would have the resources to hire MBA, which is the point of the program. It provides services for microbusinesses that need the help MBA could give them but can't afford to retain the company."

"And your colleagues don't object?"

"The program was started by MBA's founder, and I'm not the only one in the firm who participates."

"Amazing."

"We're not quite as altruistic as it might sound. A number of the companies we've mentored got big enough to need MBA's help with expansion planning."

"Still. Pretty impressive."

"So, now you don't mind cutting our date short?"

"How can I when you're off on your white horse to save a microbusiness owner from disaster?"

The memory of his father announcing at the dinner table the latest failure in a long line of business debacles, necessitating yet another move for his family, flashed through his mind. "I do the best I can."

Chapter Fourteen

There it was again. The glazed-over look. He was someplace else. One of these times, she'd figure out what brought it on and she'd know his secrets. God knows he had them.

When he walked her to the door of her apartment, he leaned in to kiss her, but this time, it wasn't the hot, passionate kiss she'd been looking forward to. It was softer, almost brotherly. Certainly distracted, like the cloudy look in his eyes. He didn't wait for her to open the door before leaving, saying, "Talk to you soon."

"Wait. I haven't thanked you." She touched his arm to stop him. "It was another lovely day. Thank you for the delicious brunch. And your guide services."

"My pleasure. Again. I enjoy showing off the city to such a receptive audience." Something in their interchange seemed to have shaken off whatever his mood had been because he smiled. "And I think we can call it what it really was, don't you?"

"Which is?" The hopeful feeling sprouted again as she waited for his answer.

"A date. I'm pretty sure it was a date."

"I was sure last weekend, but I didn't want to frighten you by insisting on calling it that."

"Knights on white horses don't frighten as easily as you seem to think we do." His blue eyes had the summer sky in them again.

"Well, then, thank you for our *date*." She went up on tiptoes and kissed his cheek, just to have a chance to be close to him, to feel his warmth and smell the aftershave he wore. He must have felt the same way because he held her close when she tried to back away.

"I'm sorry I have to leave."

She could feel his heartbeat, strong and steady against her. "I wish you could stay, too. Maybe next time."

He pulled back far enough to look at her face. "Are you saying there'll be a next time?"

"Unless you think otherwise."

He answered by returning her to a close embrace and kissing the top of her head.

Without moving from his arms, she said, "I was thinking I wanted to celebrate next week after the planning commission hearing." She could immediately feel his body become tense. When she looked up at him, he had another unreadable expression on his face.

"Yeah, I imagine you and Summer will be ready to celebrate."

"Well, yes, on Wednesday night, we'll have dinner together. I was thinking of a more personal celebration on the weekend. Maybe a two-fold deal."

"What kind of deal did you have in mind?"

"I thought I'd like to celebrate the end of our troubles with the city and to thank you for your tour guide services for the past two weekends. Maybe make dinner for us here at my place." She put her hand on his chest and looked him directly in the eye. "What do you think?" She thought she could see not just the beginning of curiosity in his expression but also the release of some of the tension that had been visible in his jaw.

"It sounds great. I mean, if it wouldn't be too much trouble."

"It would be a pleasure, not trouble. I love to cook. And I bet you've never had homemade Cuban food."

The real Taylor was fully returned in the laugh that broke out. "I've never had non-homemade Cuban food, if there is such a thing. I'd be a fool to turn down an invitation to have the real thing. What time shall I be here, and what kind of wine goes with Cuban food?"

"Be here at seven, and bring whatever you like to drink. I'm flexible and so's my food."

• • •

After months of pushing, shoving, and doing everything but laying siege to the planning department to get their zoning change, the hearing the following Wednesday went so smoothly and quickly, Bella had to wonder what all the fuss had been about.

Mrs. Pennington, the neighborhood association president, was, as they'd been told in advance, the only person testifying in opposition. She objected to the rezoning because it didn't fit into the planning documents adopted by the city and because there had already been too many commercial rezonings of residences in their neighborhood.

But Summer had done such an excellent job of presenting their proposal, complete with testimonials from their neighbors in Portland, the zoning change was granted with little discussion among the planning commissioners. The only limit was they were not to employ more than four full-time employees. The number was written into the neighborhood land use plan as a way to mitigate parking problems that might occur when businesses took over space in a residential neighborhood. Summer had already known of the restriction when she'd bought the house. Four people were more than enough to run her business, now and for the foreseeable future.

At dinner that evening, Bella and Summer celebrated their win. And strategized what the next steps were.

"What should we do about Mrs. Pennington?" Bella asked.

"I tried to talk to her after the vote, but she hightailed it out of the building before she could be trapped into a conversation," Summer responded. "I'm pretty sure she doesn't want to talk to us."

"I'll see what I can do to track her down. Maybe the city staff can help me."

"Don't waste your time," Summer said. "We won. She lost. We don't need her anymore."

"We don't need her, but it would be smart to see if we could at least neutralize her, if not get her on our side. Otherwise, every little thing we do, from painting the porch to putting up a sign, will be another opportunity for her to complain about us."

"You might be right, but I hate to see you beat your head against this particular stone wall when it could be a waste of time."

"I don't mind trying to mend fences if it makes it easier to do business in the neighborhood."

"Given how angry the woman looked after the vote was taken, this fence has a hole to mend big enough to drive a herd of cattle through," Summer said. "But have at it, girlfriend. You've done everything else you've set out to do so far. I don't doubt you can pull this off, too."

Before Summer returned to Portland the next day, Bella walked her through what would be happening to the building now that they had the zoning change. They picked out furniture, decided on a phone service, and began to plan for a formal opening. Everything was humming along nicely.

Everything except trying to track down Mrs. Pennington, Bella discovered after Summer left. She couldn't get any more traction than her boss had. There was no listing online for her. When she contacted the planning staffer she'd been working with, he wouldn't give out a phone number. The office of the city neighborhood association hemmed and hawed about giving her a contact number, saying it was against city policy to hand out personal telephone numbers. Finally, the second woman she was referred to took pity on her and made a suggestion: she'd give Bella's phone number and e-mail address to the woman in question and let her decide if she wanted to make contact. It wasn't what Bella wanted, but it was better than nothing.

In the meantime, she continued to work her way through the list of former BU/MU clients around the Puget Sound to contact for testimonials. And there were dozens of possibilities. She didn't know why she was surprised there were so many. The whole reason for Summer to expand her business had been the increasing demand for her services in this part of the Northwest.

She set up appointments with several small businesses ranging from a cupcake bakery wanting to merge with a wedding cake bakery to the founders of a cyber security firm who had worked through a way to split the firm into two distinct and noncompeting businesses when the founders had disagreements on the future of the company.

Then there were the individuals: husbands who wanted to get back together with estranged wives. Girlfriends who wanted to break it off with their boyfriends. Boyfriends who wanted to tell their boyfriends how they felt but wanted something with a bit more pizzazz than a simple "I love you."

Her favorites were the letters to and from animals: dogs that wanted to find a mate or, conversely, wanted another dog to stay out of their territory. A parakeet that needed company. There were never requests from cats, she noticed. Cats never seemed to care enough about anyone or anything else to bother to send a letter.

By the end of the day on Friday, she had appointments set for the following week with more than a dozen former clients all around the Puget Sound. She was obviously going to spend most of the week driving from Tacoma to Everett, as well as a few towns and neighborhoods around Seattle. She was looking forward to it. Traveling around for her appointments would help her get to know the area better. Taylor had inspired her to explore a little more, and she was excited about doing some of it herself, even if she'd loved having him show her around for the past few weeks.

She'd started out with an easy phone call—Allison Lindberg. She was meeting her for coffee on Monday, and she was looking forward to reconnecting with her. Not only did she hope to pick up an endorsement from Allison for their brochure but she hoped to find out what had happened with Teej.

Her satisfaction from her successful week must have bubbled over on the phone Friday evening when her brother Javier called to check in with her. Because the second thing he said, after "How you doing?" was "What's making you so happy? You find some guy or something?" Then he laughed.

Which infuriated her. It was bad enough one of her brothers called every week to check up on her. To assume only being with a guy would make her happy then to laugh at the idea she might be was too much.

"Remind me again why you're my favorite brother?" she said.

"Oh, come on, Bella. I'm joking." He paused for a moment. "Or maybe I shouldn't make a joke about something serious. Is there someone?"

"Why would it take a guy to make me happy? Why wouldn't I be happy because, oh, I don't know, maybe because my job's going well and I'm loving Seattle? How about *that* for a reason to be happy?"

"Jesus, okay. I didn't mean to make you go ballistic. So, the job's going well?"

Now he was trying to calm her down. If he'd been sitting next to her, he would have stroked her arm. "Yes, it's going great. We finally got the rezoning done, and the renovations are underway. I'm putting together a marketing brochure after I interview our clients from the area for testimonials. And I've lined up a pool of counselors, attorneys, and writers to use when the office opens in a few months. In fact, it should open in time for my birthday. Which, I might add, will be much better this year than the last one was."

There was silence at Javier's end of the call. "Are you still there?" she asked.

"Yup. I was waiting to make sure you were finished telling me how wonderful you are before I said anything."

"Oh, crap, Javier. You are so full of it."

"But I can always make you laugh, can't I?"

"Yes, you can." Now it was her turn to be quiet for a moment.

"I'm sensing there's more to this story."

She sighed. "Yes, there is. Actually, I have met someone. He's a partner with MBA Consulting, the firm we've hired to develop a marketing plan for us. He's been showing me around Seattle a little."

"I knew it. The sound of your voice practically reeked sex. What do you know about him? When did you plan to tell us about him? Where's he from? We have to meet him."

"Hold it. No sex. Not in my voice. Not in my life. He's a nice guy, from Seattle."

"Surely you know more than that about him. You can't be that naive."

Trying to deflect her brother's interest, she said, "I know Marius Hernandez likes him." At least, if Marius was willing to set her up with him, she assumed he liked Taylor.

"That's something, I guess. Maybe I'll call Marius and see what he has to say about this guy. What's his name?"

"Don't you dare call Marius."

"Okay, I'll come see you instead and make you introduce us."

"You come here, and I'll tell Sandra Daniels you're on your way and arrange for her to be here to greet you."

"That was over ... Wait. How'd you know about Sandra and me? What did she say?"

"*She* didn't say anything. But you just did." She couldn't help the smug tone to her voice. "Here's the deal, brother mine: You stay out of my life, and I won't interfere in yours."

"I don't have much choice since I have too much going on here to make good on my threat to come to Seattle anyway. And I'm not trying to interfere. We all worry about you. You're on your own for the first time in your life, and we know nothing about what you're up to. Not to mention not knowing who you're going out with. Maybe this guy's all wrong for you."

"I don't think so, but whether he is or isn't, I'll figure it out for myself. Look, Javier, I've got a job I love, and I'm doing it well. I'm living in a place I love. And I'm dating a nice guy. This is what you all told me you wanted, isn't it? So what's the problem?"

Silence again, then it was his turn to sigh. "Yeah, that's what we said. The problem is, I'm not sure until now I understood what it really meant."

Chapter Fifteen

Bella spent most of Saturday prepping for the dinner she was making for Taylor that evening. Her apartment needed serious attention before she was comfortable having anyone see the mess she'd created while she focused on work over the past few weeks. Well, work and weekends consisting of one day of fun with Taylor and another day of mooning over him like a teenager. No mooning today. Only getting things in order.

He was so tidy and neat, she wanted her place to at least appear on the surface to come up to his standard. So the morning was spent clearing away clutter then dusting, vacuuming, or scrubbing whatever she found underneath. She put clean towels out in the bathroom and, on an impulse, changed the sheets on her bed. She had no idea if they'd end the evening there—although if she had her way, they would—but she wanted to be prepared.

When she was satisfied she had it all tidied up, she hit the grocery store. She planned a completely Cuban meal, everything from the Cuba Libres she'd serve if he wanted something to drink before dinner other than wine, to the *ropa vieja* over rice and her mother's standby salad with avocados. She'd end the meal with flan. All were family favorites, and it made her happy to be making them for someone she thought would appreciate them.

Once back at her apartment, she prepped the meal and set the table. Then she took a long, hot, bubble bath to relax her. It had been so long since she entertained a date where she lived, she was a bit nervous. In the two or so years she'd lived with her parents in Portland, it wouldn't have been possible, even if she'd met someone, to invite him back to the house. In L.A., she'd shared an apartment with two college friends, making the logistics of arranging to have the space to herself complicated. Besides, most of the men she'd had over for drinks then had been more friends than potential lovers. The last time she'd had a serious boyfriend had been in college, and cooking for him meant trying to find a clean pot, dish, and fork in the old house he shared with three other guys who were as messy as he was.

This evening felt like something momentous was happening. And it made her both excited and a bit apprehensive. Not scared exactly. But certainly not sure how it would all play out.

She selected what she would wear with as much care and attention as she had paid to selecting the beef for the main dish and the avocados for the salad. Business dress wasn't appropriate, but she didn't want to be ripped-jeans-and-T-shirt casual either. She hadn't realized how lacking her wardrobe was in date-night clothes until she started looking in her closet after her shower when it was too late to run to Nordie's. She'd have to do with what was there. After trying on a half dozen possibilities, she settled on a black and white striped sweater with white skinny jeans and her black boots. With a chunky silver necklace and some small silver hoops, she thought it worked.

A half hour before Taylor was due to arrive, she looked around the apartment and was pleased with what she saw, heard, and smelled. The simmering beef filled the apartment with a delicious, spicy aroma. The place was neater than it had been in weeks and the candles on the low table in front of her couch and on the dining table would lend a romantic glow when they were lit. Playing softly in the background was her favorite music, the Buena Vista Social Club. All she needed was the man, and the evening could begin.

• • •

As he shaved, Taylor went back and forth about what to take with him to dinner at Isabella's. Even though the zoning issue had been resolved, his guilt at causing the problem for Break Up or Make Up was still nagging at him. Which led him to consider things like adding candy or a stuffed animal to the flowers and wine he'd already purchased to try to make up for what he'd done. But, of course, Isabella didn't know what he'd done, did she? He'd have to tell her first, before explaining why he arrived laden with gifts. And he knew damn well that wasn't the way he wanted to start off the evening.

Then there were the condoms staring at him from the counter beside the sink. He'd bought a box while he was out scooping up romantic presents. Now, he wasn't so sure he should take them. If he left them at home, he wouldn't be tempted to take Isabella to bed. If he took them, it would mean he had every intention of acting on the chemistry that was as obvious to her as it was to him.

But what was chemistry without trust? Didn't she deserve someone more honest and trustworthy than he was? Everything between them so far had been great. But the secret he was hiding could undo it all.

And then there was the warm and loving family she came from. Didn't she deserve to be with someone who had a similar background? Someone who would know how to treat a woman so secure in the affection of her family she beamed joy and happiness with any little thing that happened to her. God knows, he wasn't that guy. He knew how to plan, to prepare for the worst, work for the best, but expect it might fail. As much as he wished he could steal some of her glow, he didn't think it would rub off on him no matter how close he held her or for how long.

Rubbing against her. There it was again. All week long he'd thought about the implications of dinner at her apartment. Her tiny apartment where the bedroom was probably only feet away from the living room. Where even the couch would invite him to get horizontal with her, her arms and legs wrapped around him while he kissed her—everyplace.

Shake it off, Jordan. You are seriously off the rails with this woman. Get back to your plan. Don't let her get you so turned around. The reflection staring back at him from the mirror might have been nicely shaved, but the expression in his eyes said the pep talk hadn't taken. He had to face it—all he wanted to do with his attraction to Isabella was to enjoy it, his plans be damned. Now, with her troubles with the city staff over, chemistry could gain an edge over guilt. If he'd let it.

The upshot of his conversation with himself was a few condoms found their way into his wallet as he got ready to leave for Isabella's. He told himself taking them didn't mean he had to use them. But he knew he had every intention of returning home with at least one of them flushed away.

• • •

In his eagerness to see her, he got to Isabella's apartment ten minutes early. He debated waiting in his car until the appointed time, but he couldn't. Luckily, she looked happy to see him when she answered his knock.

"I'm early. Do you mind?" he said. Then fully registering what he saw, he said, "You look beautiful."

"Early is fine. Come in. And thank you for the compliment. I think I'm supposed to say 'oh, these old things' and pretend I merely threw something on. But it would be a lie. It took me forever to decide what to wear."

He was unduly pleased she had spent some time deciding on her wardrobe for the evening. "I don't know much about Cuban national dress, but I don't think that's what you're wearing."

She laughed. "No, nothing I own qualifies, but my necklace was made for me by a Cuban jewelry designer in Miami, if that counts."

"It's lovely." He touched the largest of the silver circles on the necklace, felt the heat of her through her sweater, and heard her sudden intake of breath at his touch. He pulled his hand away quickly. "I, uh, brought some wine. And flowers." He handed her his offerings. "I tried to find mariposa but ..."

"You knew that's the national flower of Cuba?" she interrupted as she took the flowers from him. "I'm amazed."

"No, I didn't. But Mr. Google knew, and he's always willing to share his information." He followed her into the kitchen. "Unfortunately, I couldn't find any in any florist shop I called."

As water filled a clear glass vase, she cut off the bottoms of the stems of the bouquet of Gerbera daisies. "I don't think I've ever seen any in the west, come to think of it. Last time I saw a mariposa was in Miami." She arranged the flowers neatly and set the vase on the counter. "Now, can I get you a drink? To follow the theme of the evening, I can make Cuba Libres or we can open the bottle of wine you brought."

"Cuba Libres. That brings back memories. I haven't had one since I was a teenager. My brother used to make them with the rum he stole from our parents. The Coke made the alcohol tolerable. Let's have one of those and save the wine for dinner. I hope red works with what you're serving."

"It's *ropa vieja*—old clothes."

"Smells awfully good for something named after Goodwill donations."

"It's shredded beef, but it's supposed to look like rags. The story goes, a poor man added old clothes to the meager meal he had for his children, and magically, it turned into beef. I think red works with either beef or rags, don't you?" She opened a cabinet above the counter next to the sink and reached for glasses that were clearly too high for her to grab. "I guess I need a stool to get the glasses."

He came up behind her. "Which ones do you want?" Her scent flooded his brain with all sorts of erotic messages—not particularly difficult to do given his internal dialogue while he shaved.

She leaned back a bit, her firm little butt brushing against him, and pointed at the top shelf. "Those, up there." Her voice sounded tight, thick. She turned to look over her shoulder at him, and her breast brushed his arm. "Do you see which ones I mean?"

"Which ones, where?" He knew exactly what she wanted, but what *he* wanted was more contact between their bodies.

She responded by stretching a bit more and pulling his hand higher, both actions increasing the friction of her body against his. "There. The tall ones."

He tried to think of some way to keep the conversation about glasses going so she wouldn't move away from him but knew that if he kept pretending he couldn't see the row of highball glasses on the top shelf, she'd wonder if he'd lost his mind.

"Got them." He snagged two glasses and brought them down. But he didn't move after he placed them on the counter. Instead he turned her around in the circle of his arms before touching her face with the palm of his hand. She leaned her cheek into his hand and sighed softly.

He couldn't stop himself. With his free hand, he drew her against him and lowered his head so he could kiss her.

• • •

Oh God, she'd wanted this since the minute she'd opened the door and seen him standing there. He looked so seriously delicious in his navy slacks and white Oxford cloth shirt. When he took off his leather jacket, she could see the golden hairs on his arms where he'd rolled the sleeves of his shirt up. She wanted to run her hand over them, find out if they were soft or crisp. Play with them. Nibble on them.

She closed her eyes, ran her hands up his arms, and felt them now. His skin was warm, the hairs soft. Every nerve in her body was doing a happy dance as he gently touched her mouth with his, then nipped at her lower lip. When she moaned, he slicked his tongue over the little bites, as if to soothe her. She could taste his toothpaste, smell his aftershave. Feel his arousal against her.

The fingers of one hand were spread along her jaw so he could tilt her head to give him a perfect fit for the kiss. The other hand slid down her bottom so he could press her hips against his. It was all she could do to keep herself from rubbing against him like a cat in heat.

He broke the kiss and murmured something—her name, she thought. Whatever it was made her shiver with anticipation. When he came back for another kiss, it wasn't soft or gentle this time. It was rougher, deeper, more passionate. She responded with all the pent-up attraction she'd felt for him since the first day she'd met him. Her nipples were in painful peaks squeezed against his chest. She knew it would only take a little encouragement, and they would be continuing this exploration in the comfort of her bedroom.

Then the timer on the stove began to buzz. It was loud, harsh, and she knew it wouldn't stop until she stopped it.

She pulled out of his arms. "I'm so sorry. It's the rice making that noise. The timer, I mean, reminding me to start the rice." She punched the button on the stove with vehemence, annoyed they'd been interrupted.

"It's okay. At the rate we were going, your dinner would be ruined." He looked around as if to find something to distract him, his gaze landing on the glasses he'd brought out of the cabinet. He grabbed them and filled them—overfilled them, really—with cubes from the icemaker. She knew how he felt. She needed something to cool her down, too. "I can finish making the drinks," he said, "while you deal with the rice, if you'll point me in the direction of your rum."

She showed him the cabinet where she kept a couple bottles of hard liquor before going about her task, grateful it didn't take anything more complicated than boiling water because after that kiss, anything else would have been impossible to do.

He kept her company in the kitchen, drinking his rum and Coke, while she finished preparing their dinner. Her ability to carry on a conversation returned, and she explained the food to him, giving him tastes of the meat and a sample of the salad dressing. The atmosphere didn't cool off much, in spite of the ice cubes and cold drinks. Turned out, feeding him was almost as sexy as kissing him. Watching him lick the spoonful of dressing she was holding for him reminded her of what it felt like when he licked her lips. His touch when he steadied the fork laden with meat she offered him ignited the same sparks all over her that his hand always did. She could tell from the way his eyes darkened, he felt it, too.

And not once did something happen to make him hide behind the mask he sometimes pulled over his face, which may have been the sexiest part of all.

The meal was a success. The wine worked perfectly with the meat. When they were finished with dessert, during which he did everything but lick the dish to get the last little bits, he insisted on helping to clear the table and load the dishwasher. After everything was tidied up, they took the last of the bottle of wine and cups of coffee into the living area and settled on the couch.

"You are an excellent cook. Everything was delicious." He touched his wine glass to hers. "Another toast to the hostess. Thank you."

"I'm happy you liked it. It's been a while since I cooked that meal. I haven't had anyone to appreciate it since my father passed. It was his favorite."

He reached for her free hand, raised it to his lips, and kissed it. "I'm honored you made it for me."

She weighed the wisdom of saying what she wanted to say but, maybe on the strength of a bit of wine, maybe because of the kiss before dinner, finally said, "I must bore you with all my family talk. You don't talk much about yours, do you?"

He dropped her hand and looked away. "There's really not much to talk about. I'm not close to them. My mother's gone. My dad lives in Spokane, and I don't see him often. I've lost touch with my brother. We weren't a happy family like yours. You were fortunate."

She slid closer to him on the couch. "I'm sorry. I didn't mean to bring up an uncomfortable subject."

"Not uncomfortable. It's just the way things are. You had the support of a family to keep you safe all the years you grew up. My father's idea of stability and planning was to make sure we had enough milk in the refrigerator at night for his coffee the next morning. Anything else was a bonus."

She could hear the hurt underneath the sarcasm. "It must have been tough on you and your brother."

"Yeah." He ran his hands over his face. "I decided at a young age to get out of there as soon as I could and never look back. My brother left in another way—he escaped into a bottle."

She couldn't help it. She put out her arms to hug him. He was tense at first, but eventually, he pulled her closer to him and returned the gesture. "You didn't deserve so much stress. No kid does," she said. Pressing a soft kiss to his cheek, she added, "So that's where all your skill at planning came from, is it?"

"I don't know about skill, but it's probably where my determination to look ahead so I can avoid problems was born."

He didn't say anything more, merely held her, his cheek resting on top of her head. She wanted to change the subject to something more comfortable for both of them. "What does your ability to look ahead tell you about the rest of this evening?" she asked.

A curl had escaped the scrunchie she'd used to try to subdue her hair. He seemed more focused on the curl than on her question. "The rest of the evening? I'm not sure I know what you mean."

"I thought I was pretty clear." She repeated herself, slowly and carefully. "What's going to happen for the rest of the evening, do you think? Between us, I mean." She looked up at him, hoping she'd see the answer she wanted in his eyes.

Instead, he asked, "What do *you* want to happen?"

It was what her brothers would call "go big or go home" time.

"I want you to kiss me again. Then I want to show you the rest of my apartment."

He looked puzzled. "A house tour? Have I missed something?"

"Yes. My bedroom."

Chapter Sixteen

For all her bravery in inviting him into her bedroom, Taylor could see Isabella was anxious when they got there. She pulled him into the room and stopped as they approached the bed. "I think I've run out of nerve. I don't know what to do next," she said as she patted the crimson blanket neatly folded on the foot of a white duvet, for the first time he could recall, avoiding looking at him.

Everything about her was open and honest, and he loved her for it. *Loved?* Wait. What? No, not possible. He admired her. That was how he felt, wasn't it? It couldn't be love. Love wasn't part of the plan. His mother had loved his father, at least at first, which had gotten her exactly nowhere.

Before he could twist himself into any more knots over her, she stepped toward him, said, "Well, maybe I can do this," and slipped her arms around his waist. With her body against him, he did the only thing he could. He tangled his fingers in her curls and drew her face to his. It was as hot and hard as the kiss in the kitchen had been, their tongues stroking intimately, tasting, exploring, deepening the passion between them.

As the kiss went on and on, his hands found their way under her sweater, skating up her back then slipping around to cup her breasts, which he was surprised to find were not confined in a bra. Her nipples were already hard points before he tweaked them, eliciting a moan from her that made his cock harder than he thought possible.

"I want you, Isabella," he whispered as he nibbled and licked his way from her mouth to her ear. She shivered when he breathed on the spot behind her ear where he'd sucked to get one more taste of her, as though he were a starving man and she was the food.

"We have to get rid of this," he said and shoved her sweater up over her head. It caught on the heavy necklace she was wearing, and untangling it momentarily dampened some of the mood as she giggled at his frustration. But once it was off and he could see the dark pink nipples waiting for him, his mouth watered in anticipation. And when he dropped to his knees and, holding her tightly by the hips, feasted on them, her laughter turned to sighs. Her moans of pleasure urged him on as he caressed, suckled, and licked first one breast then the other.

"Taylor, please. I don't think I can stand up anymore," she whispered as he indulged himself with her beautiful breasts.

Her eyes were glazed. Her body was arched toward him. Desire had taken up residence on her face, softening it, lighting it with pleasure. Seeing her like this, knowing he'd put the look there shot him from rock hard to solid steel.

"It's okay. I've got you. I won't let you go." He stood, holding her firmly with one arm, reaching around her with the other to pull down the comforter and sheet. Then he gently lowered her onto the bed. He pulled off her boots and, with her help, unsnapped and removed her jeans. The sight of her wild curls spread over the pillow, her brown eyes black with want, wearing only a bit of lace for panties and the heavy silver necklace was almost enough to push him over the edge.

"You are the most beautiful thing I've ever seen. I wish I were an artist. I would paint you like this so I could never forget you."

She reached out to him. "I need you here. Please."

He unbuttoned and shed his shirt as quickly as he could, followed by his shoes, socks, pants, and boxer briefs, all of which he carefully placed on a chair across the room. As he walked back toward her, he heard a sharp intake of breath, followed by a low moan. "It's not me who's beautiful. It's you. You're like a Viking god," she said.

On his hands and knees he scrambled across the bed to where she was lying. "Not one drop of Scandinavian blood in me, but I'm happy you like what you see."

. . .

Like what she saw? That was an understatement. He was even more delicious out of his clothes than he was in them. His shoulders were broad; his hips were slim. Dustings of golden hair were scattered over a chest with dips and valleys she wanted to run her tongue over. And the erection on display as he'd crossed the room was even more tempting. Her fingers ached, her mouth craved. She wanted to touch him, taste him.

But he had other ideas. He grabbed her hips with both hands and began to kiss his way from the valley between her breasts down to her navel, where he ran his tongue around it, then moved on to first one hipbone then across to the other, all the while kissing, licking, sucking, igniting sparks again, this time everywhere south of her waist.

Moving his hands around to her bottom, he traced more kisses down her body. As he reached her pubic hair, he stopped, looked up, and said, "If I do anything you don't like, you'll tell me, won't you?"

She couldn't get her brain cells to construct a sentence so she only nodded agreement.

"Good." He gently pushed her legs apart and settled himself between them. Watching her the whole time, he touched, just touched, her sex on the outside of her panties, and she thought she'd die from the pleasure of it. He slipped a finger under the elastic and separated her labia. "You're wet already. I like knowing you want me like this."

"Please. I want you now." Her breath was ragged; she was barely able to keep from grinding against him.

"Not yet. But soon." He slipped her panties down over her bottom and, with her help, removed them. Then he lowered his head, and his tongue went straight to the place his finger had been. She could feel the tip of his tongue circling, could feel the orgasm beginning in her until finally, as his fingers joined his tongue, she felt the earthquake begin inside her as her world fell apart and her body shattered into shards of light.

As she came down from the most amazing climax of her life, she felt the bed shift as Taylor got up. Panicked, she whispered, "No, please, don't go." She was sure she sounded desperate.

"There's no place I'm going except to get some protection from my wallet." He returned to the bed, the packet held up for her to see. She reached for it and tore it open with her teeth as soon as he gave it to her. When he was back beside her, she nudged him onto his back and unrolled the condom onto him, enjoying the chance to get her hands, finally, on his erection.

"If you take much longer, there won't be anything left to play with," he said. Rather tensely, she thought.

"Believe me, I don't plan to spoil things for either one of us," she responded. As if to prove it to him, when she was finished with her task, she straddled him. "But it's your turn now, don't you think?"

He grinned up at her. "You know I can flip you any time I want to, don't you?"

Rising up on her knees, she positioned herself over the tip of his penis. "Yes, but if you did, you'd miss this." Slowly, very slowly, she began to lower herself onto him. The hiss of breath she heard as she finally seated him completely inside her told her he was quite happy about having the tables turned.

When he grabbed her hips again, she whispered, "You like holding me like that don't you?"

"I like holding you any way I can."

Still for a moment, she eventually began to rock back and forth, then slowly up and down, leaning over him, her hair falling against his chest. She could feel him deep inside her, filling her. And when he began to massage her clitoris, she knew it wouldn't be long before she came again.

Which was enough to distract her so he could do as he had said he could. Still deep inside her, he flipped her over. As she felt her internal muscles pulse and throb around him and the world begin to shatter again, with one powerful thrust, and roaring her name, he came seconds after she did.

For a few moments, there was little heard in the room other than the sound of two people trying to catch their breath. Taylor had collapsed on her as soon as he climaxed, but eventually he moved off her. She made a small sound of protest, wanting to prolong the feeling of having him inside her, on her, surrounding her with his arms. His response was to look deeply into her eyes before rolling over so he was sitting up with his back to her. He looked stiff, tense, not at all like a man who had just had great sex.

"Taylor? Is something wrong?" she asked, afraid if she saw his face she'd see the only-too-familiar distant look.

"No, nothing's wrong. I need to get rid of this condom." He went into her bathroom without turning back to look at her and shut the door.

She pulled the comforter up over her still damp and rapidly chilling body. The scent of Taylor's aftershave mixed with the smell of sex and sweat, which she inhaled, put a smile on her face. The man who had made love to her—and it had definitely been lovemaking, not merely sex—was all she could ask for in a lover. He was tender, passionate, and he cared as much about her pleasure as his own.

Then the smile faded as she wondered if the man who left her bed for the bathroom was someone else altogether.

Chapter Seventeen

For the second time in less than twenty-four hours, Taylor was staring at himself in a bathroom mirror wondering what the hell he was doing. He thought he'd buried his guilt about his role in the problems Break Up or Make Up had with the city by rationalizing that the whole mess had been sorted out. Everything was fine. He'd even begun to believe he could tell her and they'd joke about it.

Right. Like he could joke about his dysfunctional family.

How could he have been so stupid? The look she gave him after they'd made love brought back all the guilt and shame, multiplied now by the knowledge he'd taken her to bed when she didn't really know who he was. Her big brown eyes had been full of trust and, God help him, an emotion he knew was much, much more than mere desire. He was the biggest ass in the city, in the state, if he thought he'd be able to blithely have sex with her without any consequences. Now he had to face it—he was falling for her, and from that look in her eyes, she felt the same way.

There was no way around it. He had to tell her what he'd done. Had to get it over with. If she told him to get out of her apartment, out of her life, he'd at least have been kicked to the curb knowing he'd finally been honest with her.

He splashed his face with cold water, dried his hands and face, and went back into the bedroom.

"Are you okay?" she asked. "You were gone a long time." He could hear real concern in her voice, which made it much harder to do what he was about to do.

He sat on the edge of the bed, his back to her. "I'm fine. Really. But there's something I have to tell you." He turned around to face her while he confessed.

She held up her hand and shook her head. "Don't. Please. From the look on your face, you feel like you have to tell me something bad. Unless you have some awful disease or have stashed a crazy wife in an institution someplace because you can't divorce her or you're a serial killer, I don't want to know tonight." She took his hand and kissed each knuckle individually. "This has been the most perfect night of my life, and I don't want to come down from it yet. Whatever it is you want to tell me can wait until the morning." She looked up into his face. "Can't it?"

He knew he should say it couldn't. Knew he shouldn't allow her to let him off the hook. But he did. "Okay. If that's what you want."

"It is. Now come back to bed. I need some serious spooning."

He held her the way she wanted to be held and listened as her breathing fell into a regular pattern of sleep. She was beautiful even when she slept. So beautiful it broke his heart. She deserved more than he'd given her. Hell, once he'd known who she worked for, he should never have given in to the attraction. But he had. Because for the first time in his life, doing something unexpected had felt so right.

Until it felt wrong. Like it did now.

Most of the night, for him, was spent either beating up on himself about how he'd handled things with her or crafting ways to tell her what he needed to tell her in a favorable way. He was only successful at the first. He was certainly not successful at getting any sleep.

Finally, at six thirty, he gave up, disentangled his arm from around her, and inched his way off the bed. Dressing quickly in the dark, he hoped to leave before she awakened, but she must have sensed his absence from her bed because as he was finishing tying his shoes, he heard, "Taylor? Why are you getting dressed? What time is it?"

"It's almost seven. I need to go home. I was going to leave a note. It's work. You don't have to get up. I can find my way out. I'll call you. Promise." He left before she could try to convince him to stay.

• • •

"I swear to God I'm beginning to think Taylor Jordan has some kind of multiple personality disorder. One minute he's Mr. Good Guy, the next he's Mr. Gone Guy." Bella and Summer had finished their weekly Skype session and transitioned into catching up with each other's personal life.

"So the weekend didn't go the way you wanted it to?" Summer asked.

"Well, technically, part of the weekend did. Saturday was wonderful. The dinner was delicious. We talked and talked. He was sweet and funny, even talked about his family a little. Not once did he disappear behind that look he gets sometimes. I thought we were making progress."

"I hear no mention of the good stuff."

"Oh, there was good stuff. While we were getting drinks before dinner, he kissed me so thoroughly I thought we were going to end up naked on the kitchen floor." She hesitated, not sure how much she really wanted to share with her boss.

"From your hesitation, I'm guessing you are trying to figure out how to tell me you eventually did end up naked."

"I keep forgetting how good you are at understanding what *isn't* being said. Yes, he spent the night. It was amazing. I'm not the world's most experienced woman when it comes to sex, but I'm pretty sure he'd be at the top of any woman's list of fantastic lovers."

"One point in his favor, a big one, at least in my book. If Saturday was so great, what happened Sunday to turn the weekend around?"

"I wish I knew. At some God awful early hour Sunday morning, he snuck out of bed and got dressed. I woke up as he was leaving, and all he said was he had work to do. He didn't even kiss me goodbye." She could feel the tears she'd been holding back for more than a day begin to well up. She sniffled. "Sorry. I need to get a tissue." A few minutes later, she was back. "Didn't mean to be so goopy about this. I just wish I understood him better."

"Girlfriend, every woman alive has sung some verse of that song at least once in her life. Surely after all the clients you've seen come through our office, you know that."

"I guess I do. But I didn't ever think I'd be one of them."

"We never do. Have you thought about confronting him with your questions and keeping at him until he answers them?"

"I'm not sure I'd call it confronting, but I have asked him about things—his family, mostly."

"Maybe it's time for a more serious intervention. If you want to keep this relationship going, I mean."

"Yes, I want to keep it going. I've never been this attracted to a man in my life. And when things are good, they're so good it makes me wonder how I got so lucky. In fact ..." She stopped before she revealed any more.

"In fact, if I'm reading your expression correctly, you're falling for him, aren't you?" Summer asked.

Something else Bella had apparently forgotten—they were Skyping and her boss could see her face.

"I think you have the tense of the verb wrong. It should be past tense. I've already fallen for him."

"Then we better think of some ways to see if you can make this work. How about ..."

The front door to the BU/MU office opened, and Bella lost the rest of the advice her boss was giving her as the man in question walked in. He hesitated, then took a couple steps into the reception area before stopping again.

"Uh, Summer, someone's here. Maybe we could continue this conversation later."

"Sure, but don't put off taking care of this. I don't want to see you …"

"Talk to you later." She closed the Skype app before Summer could finish the sentence. "Taylor. What're you doing here?"

Somehow the fact he looked embarrassed made her feel good. "Uh, well, I thought I'd drop in and say hello. See your new place." He was actually shuffling his feet and glancing down at the floor as he spoke.

"How nice of you. Is this a service MBA offers to all its clients?"

He finally looked at her. "No, Isabella. This has nothing to do with MBA. Truthfully, it has nothing to do with seeing your new space, either. I came to apologize. And to talk to you."

"Really? Apologize for what?" She knew she was being a little mean, but after all the uncertainty he'd put her through, she was going to make him say exactly what he meant.

"For Saturday night—well, actually Sunday morning, I guess. I shouldn't have left the way I did. You deserve better." He indicated a chair next to the desk where she was sitting. "Can I sit down?"

"Are you going to be here long? Or do you have to leave for some work reason?"

He grimaced. "I deserve the barb. Actually I deserve more. Because of … well, what I want to tell you. There's another part of why I'm here. I said Saturday night I needed to tell you something. I want to get it out on the table. It may change things between, us but I have to get it out."

"Okay, sit then."

He sat but didn't look comfortable. "Would it be possible to get a cup of coffee? I need a little more caffeine than usual this morning."

What could he possibly have to tell her that took caffeine courage? "Sure. I started the coffee brewing before my Skype meeting with Summer. It should be ready by now."

•••

He watched her as she walked to what had been the old dining room and pulled out two mugs. He was mesmerized by the grace with which she did everything including something as simple as pouring coffee or adjusting the volume on the radio. Which she was now doing, muting the sound of what he thought was a local radio advice columnist. He seemed to remember she liked to listen to that program.

Maybe she'd been listening hoping for advice on how to deal with him. He didn't blame her if she was. He'd spent the entire time he'd known her going back and forth between being attracted to her beauty and easy grace, her enthusiasm for life, and her intelligence and trying to make himself run for the hills because of what he'd kept hidden from her.

No more. He was here to tell the truth. It had taken all the nerve he had to come to her office today because he knew he could be about to ruin his chances to be with her. It sucked to be honest, but it was worse to feel guilty.

"Taylor, do I remember right, you take one sugar with your coffee?" She sounded like she'd already asked the question at least once.

"Sorry. One sugar. Right."

For the first time since he had walked into the building, he saw a smile on her face. It wasn't much of one and was more sad than happy, as if she'd expected he wouldn't be paying attention, but it was something. He hoped she'd still be wearing any smile at all when he was finished telling his story.

While he'd been chewing over the same shreds of guilt and fear he'd been working on all weekend, she'd apparently been standing in front of him with a mug of coffee extended to him, her sad look still in place. "Thanks," he said. He took a huge swig and nearly choked on it.

She returned to her chair on the opposite side of what he assumed would one day be the receptionist's desk. "So," she started, "you had something you wanted to tell me."

He took another gulp of coffee. "It's kind of a long story," he began. "A year or so ago ..."

The office phone rang. She looked frustrated at the interruption. Saying, "I'm sorry, I have to answer this," she picked up the phone. "Good morning. This is Bella at Break Up or Make Up. How can I help you?"

He saw her eyes light up when the person at the other end of the call responded.

"Mrs. Pennington, I'm so glad you called. I've wanted to touch base with you ever since the planning commission hearing. I hoped we could try to iron out our differences so we can be a positive part of what's going on in the neighborhood."

Oh, shit. Jane Pennington was on the other end of the call. The woman he'd gossiped to who started the snowball rolling that almost buried Isabella and Summer in an avalanche. And Isabella wanted to talk to her. Double shit. He slammed the mug down so hard the remains of his coffee slopped over the edge onto his hand and the papers on the desk.

She continued, "Coffee would be great. Let me go get my calendar, and we'll set something up." She put the phone down and disappeared into the back.

He'd known walking into the BU/MU office, it wouldn't take much to turn things into a real disaster. And now a simple phone call had done it. Isabella would think he only told her his secret because Mrs. Pennington was about to out him over a cup of Starbucks's finest.

His last bit of courage was gone. He had to be, too. He wrote a note saying he'd gotten a call from his office and had to go and slipped out the front door before Isabella came back. The chance of explaining what he'd done in a way that didn't look petty and stupid had been slim to begin with. On the slim-to-none scale, he'd now officially reached "none."

Chapter Eighteen

He'd disappeared. Again. At least this time, he left a note. Summer was right. She was going to have to trap him in his office and force him to answer her questions. If he wouldn't, she was done. This was absurd. It didn't matter how attractive he was or how good he made her feel in bed. If he wasn't willing to talk about what the hell was going on and why he kept disappearing, mentally or physically, she was giving up. Surely love shouldn't be this difficult, should it?

Luckily she had a full day of meetings with former BU/MU clients to see if she could get testimonials from them about the services they'd received. She was looking forward to meeting the people she'd contacted, most of whom she'd only previously known through Summer's descriptions.

First up was a woman who'd asked for a letter from her dog to the pooch next door, trying to keep the big dog from laying claim to the smaller dog's domain. Apparently Bella's letter, which she'd run through many drafts to make sure it was funny and not offensive, had done the job. The big dog had left the little guy alone after getting the missive. Then she was dropping in on a small business owner who had used them to negotiate an amicable split with a partner, followed by a meeting with the partner from whom the owner had split.

But the meeting after was the one she was really happy about. She was having coffee with Allison Lindberg, the ex-girlfriend of the infamous Dear John Ranter. She could hardly wait to find out what had happened with that unhappy guy.

...

Bella got a bit lost in Bellevue trying to find the office building where Allison's engineering firm was headquartered, but she'd left plenty of time to get there because she was unfamiliar with the area, so she made it to the Starbucks where they were to meet on time. Allison was already in line, about to order her coffee.

"Bella, how nice to finally meet you in person. Welcome to Bellevue," Allison said. "Did you have any trouble finding the building?"

"Not really," Bella said, fudging the truth. "I wandered a bit but not too much." She waved her Starbucks card at the barista. "I'll get hers and a macchiato for me, please."

"You didn't have to treat," Allison said.

"You're doing me a favor. It's my pleasure."

They collected their coffees and settled at a corner table.

"So," Allison began. "You're opening an office for Break Up or Make Up in Seattle."

"We are. And we're contacting some of the clients we've served in the Puget Sound area to see if we can get testimonials for our marketing materials." When it looked like Allison was about to interrupt, Bella said, "We're not looking to use names, particularly for individuals. We'd use generic descriptors, like, 'woman requesting love letter for boyfriend' or 'business owner trying to repair damaged relationship with partner.'"

"Good. Because I wouldn't want my name out there as someone who broke up with her boyfriend with a letter someone else wrote for her. No matter how great I think your company is, I'm a bit embarrassed I had to resort to using you instead of doing it myself."

"Like we always say, why do it yourself and use the wrong words when you can have the professionals find the right words."

"And you did. You were wonderful."

"So, can we get a sentence or two from you saying that?"

"Let me give it some thought. I have your e-mail. If I decide to participate, I'll contact you."

"Fair enough." Bella sipped at her coffee. "Actually, asking you to give us a testimonial is only half the reason I wanted to see you. The other half is pure curiosity. I was in the office the day your ex came roaring in threatening Summer. I didn't see him, but I sure heard him. Did he ever contact you?"

"No, he cooled off I guess. I haven't seen him or heard from him since you delivered the letter. I don't suppose Taylor ... uh ... Teej took my advice and used your services, too, did he? He's a great guy, but he needs to figure a way to live life outside the straitjacket of his ambitions."

She wasn't sure she'd heard Allison correctly. "What did you call him?"

"Teej? It's the nickname I called him. I addressed his letter that way, remember?"

"Before you called him Teej, you called him something else."

Allison scrunched her face up. "Oops. Slipped, didn't I? I said his real name. It's Taylor. I called him Teej because he always signed his e-mails and texts to me with his initials: TJ."

"Taylor J?" Every instinct in her body was at DEFCON One. The roaring in her ears was louder than the sound of the Air Force scrambled for an imminent attack. "What does the J stand for?" she asked, sure her voice was quivering.

"I'm not sure I want to say. I've tried to protect his identity in all this with you."

"If I guess right, would you confirm it?" She hoped she was wrong, but she had to know.

"I suppose so. As long as you're not planning to ask him for a testimonial."

"No, that's not the reason I'm asking." She was clutching her pen so hard it hurt her fingers. "Is the J for Jordan?"

She couldn't tell from her face if Allison was surprised or suspicious. She supposed it could be both. "Yes. Do you know him?"

"Assuming he's the Taylor Jordan who works for MBA Consulting, yes, you could say I know him. Summer hired his firm to develop a marketing plan for us. They're the ones who suggested we collect testimonials."

"Oh, my God. Taylor's not working on your account, is he?"

"No, Nate Benjamin is. But I've had contact with Taylor. Run into him a few times, in the office, I mean." She was afraid she was blushing at the way she was presenting her acquaintance with Taylor. "He knows his firm is working with us. I wonder why he's never said anything about getting one of our letters?"

Allison shrugged. "Maybe he was embarrassed about it. Or maybe it was his male ego not wanting to admit to being dumped by mail."

Or maybe his goal was to embarrass BU/MU, and being honest wouldn't achieve his goal. "Well, anyway, I'm glad it turned out okay for you." She closed her small notebook and put her pen back in her purse, hoping Allison would take it as a sign the interview was over. Now that she had this bombshell information, all she wanted to do was have a chance to process it. Alone.

Allison checked the time on her phone. "Sorry to cut this short. I have to get back upstairs. Big project coming to an end, and we're all running around trying to tie up loose ends." She put out her hand. "I'll give some thought to writing up a sentence or two for you to use and get in touch."

Bella sat at the table after Allison left trying to sort out what she'd learned. Was this the big secret Taylor was hiding from her and the reason why the shutters came down over his eyes every now and then? Shouldn't he have told them when they hired his firm? Shouldn't Nate have told them? Maybe he didn't know. That had to be it. Not only had Taylor kept the secret of how Allison had broken up with him from her but he'd kept it from everyone.

She couldn't help wondering if this was some part of Taylor's—no, Teej's—threat to get even. Was he playing with her so he could hurt her like he'd been hurt? Was he spying on Summer's operation by flirting with her?

On the other hand, he did try to tell her something on Saturday night and this morning in her office. Was it this? It better be. If there was something else and he intended to continue to keep this a secret ...

No way was he escaping one hell of a conversation as soon as she could arrange it. In the meantime, she had to get back to her office. She had one more coffee date this afternoon—with Mrs. Pennington, the neighborhood association president. Unlike the others today, it was not a meeting she had been looking forward to. But after the coffee date with Allison, it began to look better and better. How much worse could meeting with the Dragon Lady of the neighborhood association be?

Chapter Nineteen

Bella had invited the neighborhood association president to come to the BU/MU office, wanting to show her how carefully they'd renovated the building, fitting their office into the space with little change to the distinctly Victorian touches in the living room and dining room. Only in what had been a library were there any substantial changes—shelves had been converted to file drawers with fronts to match the existing wood and a storage closet added where none had been.

She was slightly nervous about this meeting. Mrs. Pennington hadn't been particularly friendly on the phone, although she hadn't put up any argument about meeting. Busying herself with making a fresh pot of coffee, she tried to take her mind off what the conversation might be like.

At four sharp, Mrs. Pennington appeared at BU/MU. Bella had left the inside door open so all her visitor had to do was open the screen door and come in. Instead, Mrs. Pennington paused on the porch, then knocked, as thought she were visiting a friend's home, not a business office. Bella went to the door to welcome her.

"I'm Isabella Rodriguez, Mrs. Pennington. Please, come in. You'll have to forgive the mess. We're still in the renovation stage. The workers are beginning in the kitchen this week while they finish the earthquake upgrades and the storage in the back." She led the older woman to what had once been the living room and would soon be the reception area. "I'm afraid a desk chair and a desk for our coffee is all I can offer you. The other furniture won't be here for a week or so."

"A desk chair is fine," Mrs. Pennington said. "And I take my coffee black."

Her guest settled herself on the visitor side of the receptionist desk. Mrs. Pennington was probably in her sixties with beautiful pure white hair in soft waves around her face. She was dressed in designer casual clothes and had the self-assurance and composure Bella recognized as coming from a life of privilege and security.

She fixed two mugs of coffee and returned to the desk. "I didn't really have a chance to meet you at the planning commission hearing."

Mrs. Pennington sipped at her coffee and said nothing.

"So, I'm happy you agreed to talk with me. I'm hopeful we can get a few misunderstandings straightened out."

"I was surprised when the woman from the city called to tell me you wanted to talk. I can't imagine what we have to discuss. I lost. You won." She shrugged her shoulders and sipped more coffee.

"I prefer to think, however you view the outcome of the planning commission hearing," Bella said, "we both care about the future of this neighborhood. I hope you agree with that even though we might not agree on the details of how it would all play out."

"That, my dear, is an understatement."

There was some more coffee sipping and a bit of silence before she tried again to engage her visitor in conversation. "I was hoping you'd be willing to work with us, instead of against us, as long as we're going to be in the neighborhood."

"And do what exactly?"

"I'm not sure yet. But clearing the air would be a good first step, don't you think?"

"I suppose so. How would you propose we go about clearing the air?"

"Maybe, if you're willing, you could give me some more details about why you were so adamantly opposed to our being here. I might be able to ease some of your concerns."

Mrs. Pennington said nothing for several long moments. "I suppose it wouldn't hurt to tell you. It's moot now, since the hearing. There were several reasons. The general one, the one we stated at the hearing, was that I'm opposed—the neighborhood association is opposed—to rezoning any residence for commercial use. We've already seen a great many of our older homes converted, and it's my goal—the goal of the neighborhood association—to stop any more conversions before we lose the character of the neighborhood. This is a very special residential area, and the creeping commercialization of our side streets is of concern to us. Commercial uses belong on main arterials. But on the side streets, we'd prefer to see it remain completely residential."

"I understand. It's the same problem in almost every city experiencing growth. My family is in the real estate business in California, and we deal with the issue all the time."

"Is your family in the residential or commercial end of the business?"

"Both. One brother heads up the residential side, another our commercial activities."

"You must have some interesting family dinners." For the first time, Mrs. Pennington seemed to soften up, her mouth fighting hard not to smile.

"Mrs. Pennington, I have four older and extremely bossy brothers. Even without the obvious business conflicts, we have interesting family dinners."

The older woman actually laughed. "I don't envy you four brothers. I had a hard enough time with only one."

"Well, fortunately, I'm in Seattle and they're in California so it's easier than it was when we were all in one city." She pointed to Mrs. Pennington's now empty mug. "Can I freshen your coffee?"

"Yes, thank you."

When she'd refilled both mugs, she went back to the subject of the rezoning hearing. "You said there were several reasons for your position. Can you tell me what the other reasons were?"

"We heard your company had created problems with their neighbors in Portland."

"Who told you that, if you don't mind telling me?"

"Someone from another neighborhood association who had done some research on your company. He wasn't impressed with what he'd found."

"Did he give you any specifics about the so-called problems with our neighbors?"

"Well, one of the problems was parking."

She had a hard time controlling herself so she didn't laugh. "I'm afraid problems with parking are endemic to Northwest Portland where our office is."

"It was from all those people coming and going at all hours."

"Actually, we don't have people coming and going, even during regular business hours. One of the reasons the four-person limit on staff in the rezoning for this building isn't a problem is we only have a full-time staff of two in our Portland office. The counselors, social workers, and attorneys affiliated with the business are on a consulting basis and meet with our clients in their offices, not ours. Not even our freelance writers come into the office very often. They do most of their work electronically."

"That was certainly not the impression my source gave."

"What else did your source tell you about us?" she prodded, hoping for more details.

"It wasn't clear exactly what your business was. From the little we heard, it frankly sounded sordid, and we didn't want an undesirable business in the neighborhood under any circumstances. If I remember correctly, Mr. Jordan said you were involved in some questionable activities related to sexually explicit communications. Something akin to the sleazy personal ads in the tabloid newspapers."

DEFCON One reappeared, this time twisting her stomach into a knot and starting a blinding pain in her head. "Mr. Jordan? Not Taylor Jordan, by any chance?"

"Yes, do you know him?"

In every sense including the biblical. "We've met, yes. But he never mentioned he'd had contact with anyone about us."

"It was only one conversation. And he did, now that I think about it, call me later to say he was sure your company was a reputable one. But by then, we'd already officially objected. Even if he hadn't warned us about your business, we would have asked to testify at the hearing because of the reason I stated earlier, but his opinion made it even more imperative that we intervene. So we did, both with the city and in the press."

It took all the mental discipline Bella had to stay in her chair and say, in a rational tone of voice, "Given what you've told me, I understand why you might wonder about what we do. Especially since I'm not aware of any company like us anywhere else to compare us to, although I'm surprised Mr. Jordan wasn't a bit more knowledgeable. Can I tell you something about us to see if I can set your mind at ease?"

When Mrs. Pennington nodded, Bella described for her, in a few sentences, what they did and how they did it. She used examples from the list she'd pulled out of the client files and assured the woman their work was above board and, according to their clients, a needed and much appreciated service.

"I wish you'd come to me before this," Mrs. Pennington said when Bella was finished. "It might have made a difference in what we did."

"We tried. I tried. But I couldn't get the city staff to give me your contact information. Besides, they told me you were out of town."

"At least we've had this chance to get things sorted out before you open your doors for business." She rose from the chair with all the grace of a monarch leaving her throne. "Thank you for making the effort."

As she accompanied her visitor to the door, Bella said, "One last thing. I'd like to invite you to our official opening. We're hosting an open house in July. Would you be willing to be here, to show the neighbors and the press there are no hard feelings? It would mean a great deal to us."

"Send me an invitation, and I'll attend if my schedule allows. It's the least I can do when you've gone out of your way to make sure I'm—we're—comfortable with your business."

For a good five minutes after Mrs. Pennington left, Bella stood staring out the front door. She didn't know how she'd held it all together for the last part of their meeting. She felt Taylor's betrayal deep in her gut. It was clear now he had no intention of having a relationship with her. He'd played her like a violin to get back at Summer and BU/MU, just as he'd threatened to do that day in Portland. She'd been mistaken to believe the warm and approachable Taylor was the real one and the hesitant and distant mask he hid behind the false one. It was the opposite. He may not have known whom she worked for when he first saw her and there may be some truth to his saying he found her attractive, but the bigger truth was, as soon as he found out she worked for Summer, he obviously thought he'd found a way through her to track the damage his lie to Mrs. Pennington had caused.

When the thought crossed her mind that he didn't have to hook up with her to do that, that he could have found out through MBA, she rejected it. He was too methodical to rely solely on his colleague to give him the information he wanted. He wanted to be able to gloat by hearing the information from someone who was hurt by it.

This was what he had been hiding. It had to be the secret he was keeping. He may have been willing to tell her about Allison and the letter but she was sure he had no intention of ever telling her about Mrs. Pennington.

Then another piece fell into place. Oh my God. *That's* why he'd left her office on Monday! He heard her say the name of the neighborhood association president and panicked.

If he'd thought he had reason to panic then, wait until she confronted him tomorrow. Panic would be the least of his reactions.

Chapter Twenty

Fueled with a giant cup of leaded coffee to sharpen her brain and a healthful breakfast to fuel her body, Bella was ready to take on the world—or at least, Taylor Jordan's corner of it. She could hear the "Ride of the Valkyries" playing in her head as she charged off the elevator at the MBA office building like someone on a mission, which, come to think of it, she was. Blowing by the receptionist with only a cursory nod, she headed straight for Taylor's office. But once again, when she wanted to see him, he wasn't there.

If he thought he could avoid her by not being there, he was mistaken. Not knowing she wanted to see him was no excuse. At this point, everything he did was wrong, and she would wait to tell him. In detail.

It shouldn't be too long a wait. He must be in the office someplace. His suit jacket was hanging on the back of his chair, and his messenger bag was on the floor next to his desk. He never left the building without either of those things. She settled herself in his visitor's chair. It occurred to her it would serve him right if she rummaged around in his desk drawers to see what else he was hiding, but she restrained herself. She was not about to lose the moral high ground she had claimed yesterday when she found out about his deception.

He was reading something when he walked through the door and didn't see her for a few seconds. When he did, he looked, well, the only word she could think of was "hunted."

She had a feeling he knew why she was there.

The feeling was confirmed when he avoided her eyes. "Isabella. I wasn't expecting you." A last chance possibility apparently occurred to him. "Are you here to meet with Nate?"

"No. I'm here to see you."

All hope died from his face. Still not looking directly at her, he went to his desk but didn't sit down. Whether it was a signal he didn't want her to stay long or a sign he was thinking about a quick exit, she didn't know. "What can I do for you?" he finally asked.

"Well, let's see. Why *am* I here?" She knew she was being mean to drag it out, but she got great pleasure from doing so. "Oh, now I remember. I had a question or two for you after meeting with a former client of ours in Bellevue and Mrs. Pennington. I think you know her, she's a neighborhood association president."

He dropped into his desk chair. "You had a meeting in Bellevue, too?"

"Ah, I can see you're beginning to put the pieces together."

"If you'll give me a chance, I can explain, Isabella. I swear I can." He sounded tired. Or resigned, as if he'd been waiting for this particular shoe to drop for a long time.

"Explain what? How you lied to me? Kept secret the fact you're the one responsible for the problems we had with the city because of what you told Mrs. Pennington? I don't need an explanation for that. She got me up to speed on the subject quite nicely, thank you."

"I made a couple of unfortunate offhand comments at a neighborhood association summit meeting, and she ran with it. I tried to get her off the scent but ..."

"Yes, I know. It was too late to call it off. She told me that, too."

"I wasn't trying to cause trouble. It was only a casual conversation."

"A casual conversation? I'm not sure I'd call talking to our neighbors in Portland and leading Mrs. Pennington to believe we're involved in some sort of sex ring casual conversation."

"I never said anything about a sex ring. She came up with that all on her own." Now he sounded more like a petulant little boy.

"But you did tell her we had problems with our neighbors, didn't you? When you knew it wasn't true."

"Well, a couple of them said there were parking problems around your offices."

"For God's sake, there are parking problems all over Northwest Portland."

"I know. I wasn't thinking."

"Wasn't thinking or didn't care?" She waved him off when it appeared he was about to answer the question. "And wasn't it convenient of me to show up so you could have a way to keep track of how well your revenge on BU/MU was going? The revenge you vowed for the letter Allison sent you. A letter, which by the way, in case you don't already know this part, I ghosted for her."

"Oh, shit."

"My feelings exactly." She sprang from the chair and began to pace. "I have never felt so used, so played, so angry with anyone in my life."

"Please, let me explain."

"Stop it. Not only are you repeating yourself but there's no way you can explain away what you did. How did you rationalize not telling me about Allison and Mrs. Pennington?"

"I tried to. On Saturday."

"Oh, yes. After you fucked me."

"It wasn't like that, and you know it."

"Wasn't it? I feels like that to me."

"It wasn't fucking. We made love. And it was amazing. Deny it and you're the liar." He said it with conviction and certainty.

Even as mad as she was at him, she couldn't.

Her silent agreement with his statement seemed to give him the strength to continue with more conviction in his voice. "I wanted to confess the whole mess to you then, but you stopped me because you said it was the best night of your life."

"Yeah, well, I've reconsidered *that* opinion, believe me." She stopped pacing in front of his desk, braced herself on her fists, and stared hard at him. "If you had any real intention of being honest, you wouldn't have let me talk you out of it. You'd have insisted on telling me. But no. You wanted to feel like you were the good guy without having to actually do anything to earn the title. Besides, if you confessed, you'd lose your chance for revenge. And, boy, did you get back at us because you were pissed at your ex. You tied up Summer's money and my time for months and kept us chasing our tails. You almost screwed up the best job I've ever had. And to top it off, you made me look like a fool for falling for you ... for your line of bullshit, that is. You are a genuine, first-class, lying bastard, and I want nothing more to do with you."

She turned to leave, but he was on the other side of the desk faster than she imagined he could move, grabbing her arm to detain her. "Wait. Please. Let me try to explain how it happened. I didn't mean to hurt you. Hell, I didn't even really mean to hurt Summer's business."

"Let go of me. Now." She pushed at him, and he did. "I don't believe a word you're saying. I heard you in Summer's office. I was there the day you came in bellowing like a wounded bull. You wanted revenge for Allison's letter. You figured a way to get it without having your fingerprints all over it. End of story."

"What you're saying is not true. It's simply not true."

She sighed. "You know what? Whether it's true or not doesn't matter anymore. Every time we were together, it was obvious you were hiding something or were afraid of something. I thought, if I could figure it out, we could make something out of this relationship. But I was wrong. We can't. No relationship works without trust. And I can't trust you to tell the truth. I'm done. I don't want to see you or hear from you again."

Before he could stop her, she was out the door, striding for the elevator. She wasn't surprised or even upset when he didn't follow.

• • •

Taylor knew he wouldn't get anywhere going after her even though he wanted to. He'd been unsuccessful getting her to listen to him while she was in his office, and the chances he could do any better in the hall weren't good.

Instead, he waited for the twenty-five minutes he knew it would take her to return to her office, then called. He got voicemail and left a message. He texted. No response. He e-mailed. Same. He called her cellphone. Different voicemail message but message all the same. Two messages on each voicemail later, he gave up hoping she would talk to him.

Then it occurred to him maybe she wasn't answering because something had happened to her. Maybe she'd been distracted or upset by their confrontation. Suppose she'd gotten into a wreck because of him? He'd never forgive himself. He had to find out if she was okay, even if she wouldn't speak to him.

The only person he could think of who might help was Summer. It wasn't the easiest call to make, but he made it.

"Taylor. My receptionist says this is an emergency. What's going on? It's not Bella, is it?"

"I don't know what's going on. That's why I'm calling. I need your help." He wasn't sure how to broach the subject but he had to make a stab at it. "Um ... we had a bad conversation this morning ... Isabella and I ... and ... ah ... I hurt her. She's mad at me, left here steaming. I'm worried about her and she's not answering my phone calls or texts. I don't know if it's because she doesn't want to talk to me or ... "

"I talked to her fifteen minutes ago. She was on her way to an appointment. She was a bit abrupt but otherwise sounded fine."

"That would have been after she was here. At least she was okay then." He dropped into his chair, somewhat relieved.

"Out of curiosity, what could have been so horrible about a conversation you had to make you worry she'd get hurt after she left?"

"It's a little hard to explain."

"Try."

"You know she's been doing interviews with former clients for your marketing materials. Yesterday she found out my ex-girlfriend hired you to write a letter breaking off our relationship."

"Really?"

"That's only part of it. I'm embarrassed to say I'm the guy who came into your office and yelled at you about the letter his girlfriend sent him."

"Oh, my God. You're the Dear John Ranter?" He was slightly offended that Summer sounded like she was muffling laughter. When she had herself under better control, she asked, "So that's what you two argued about?"

"Mostly she yelled at me for not telling her." He paused and cleared his throat before continuing. "There was one more thing. She ... um ... found out I was the person who accidentally told Mrs. Pennington you had problems with your neighbors, which encouraged her to object to your zoning change."

Summer wasn't laughing now. "So, that's what you decided to do to make good on your threats, was it?"

"I didn't do anything deliberate. Well, I did talk to some of your neighbors before I left Portland, but by the time I got back to Seattle, I knew I wouldn't be doing anything to back up what I said to you."

"And yet you did."

"Accidently. It was a casual conversation with someone who was willing to grab at anything to stop a business from coming into the neighborhood. I didn't mean for it to go so far. And once I realized what Mrs. Pennington was doing, I tried to stop her, but the process had already been set in motion and she wasn't willing to give up."

"What else?"

"What do you mean, what else? I kept two big things from Isabella, and now she's furious. Isn't that enough?"

"Yes, but I want to make sure I have the whole story before I talk to her again. I'll call her when I know she's finished with the appointment to check in with her, if you swear that's all you've kept from her ... from us."

"Thank you. Yes, that's all."

"I wish we were on Skype so I could see your face. I think I hear sincerity in your voice, but I'd like to see it on your face. Maybe I can get at it this way: How do you feel about her?"

"What do you mean?"

"Damn it, Taylor, I mean do you love her?"

"Yes."

"Well, that was said without hesitation or qualification. Have you told her?"

"No, I wanted to tell her about Allison and Mrs. Pennington first."

"Which brings up the question of why you didn't."

"I was afraid she'd hate me if she knew about it before she had a chance to get to know me. I thought if I waited until we knew each other better, she'd be more willing to understand. But it backfired. She heard it from Allison and Mrs. P before I had a chance to tell her."

"Not the choice I would have made were I in your shoes, but at least you thought about it." She paused for a moment. "Okay, I'll help you. What do you want me to do?"

"Make sure Isabella's okay." How many times was he going to have to say it?

"Yes, I know. But what else? What can I do to help *you*?"

"Why would you want to help me?"

"It's what I do, Taylor."

"It's nice of you, but I think I'm beyond help. She's so angry she'll never speak to me again."

"You could be right, but let me think about it and get back to you. It may not be too late."

•••

Bella saw the name on the caller ID and knew it was safe to pick up. "Summer. You were next on my list to call. Hold on a minute while I turn down the radio." She muted the advice program she always listened to and returned to the phone call. "I have some news for you."

"From your appointments this week?"

"Yup. Interesting stuff." She filled her boss in on the progress of the testimonial interviews she'd had, including the surprise from Allison Lindberg, then hit her with the information she got from Mrs. Pennington. Summer took it better than she expected.

"It sucks about Taylor. You must have been devastated."

"Yeah, well, I'm over it. Easy come, easy go."

"I know ... you know ... that's not true."

"It has to be this time. I can't trust him."

"At least you solved the puzzle of what happened. And got Mrs. Pennington settled down."

She was happy to get the conversation off the subject of Taylor Jordan. "I think I even got her to agree to show up at the open house."

"Which reminds me, how about we schedule the date for the official opening right now? I was thinking, Saturday the thirteenth of July looks like a good day for a celebration, don't you think?"

Since she hadn't been sure what she would be doing on her birthday, Bella was only too happy to have a focus for the day. "Sounds good to me. What did you have in mind? Other than getting someone relevant to cut the ribbon and serving something special to our guests."

"How about a birthday cake? Is that special enough?"

"You remembered. What's wrong with me? Of course you did. It's nice of you to want to celebrate my birthday, but I thought this was to mark the grand opening of your new office."

"*Our* new office. The other thing I'd like to celebrate is the appointment of you as the program director of our Seattle office."

"Oh, my God. I hoped you'd ask. I would so love to stay here and manage this branch. You couldn't have picked a better day to offer me the job. Thank you."

"You earned it, girlfriend. So, get yourself some new business cards. A nameplate for your desk, if you'd like. And your first official job as the new director is to put together a proposal for what we need for the party with a budget I—*we*—can afford. E-mail it to me in the next couple days. I'll e-mail you a proposed contract with salary and benefits for you to consider, and we'll talk."

"Thank you so, so much. You are the best boss in the world!"

"Save the praise until you see what I'm offering you." She paused before adding, "Is there anything else you need to talk about?"

"No, nothing I can think of." Nothing she *wanted* to think of.

"Okay. If you're sure." Summer's voice softened. "Bella, after all you found out about Taylor and the whole mess with Allison and Mrs. Pennington, you're okay, aren't you? You know you can always talk to me about anything, don't you?"

"I'm fine. Don't worry about me. I'll survive."

• • •

"Taylor? Summer Olsen. I just talked to Bella. She told me about Allison and Mrs. Pennington so now I'm officially in the loop.

She's okay, determined not to be sad about what she found out, but okay."

"Thank you. I appreciate your checking in on her."

"Which brings me to my next question—do you want to get her back?"

"Of course I do, but I have a snowball's chance in hell of accomplishing that."

"Maybe not. I got an idea when I was talking to her. It'll require you stepping outside your comfort zone, but if you're willing to do it ..."

"I'll do anything. Tell me."

"Okay, then, here's my idea ..."

Chapter Twenty-One

The next few weeks went by more quickly than Bella would have imagined, given the empty place in her life where Taylor used to be. In a short time, he'd come to be so important to her, and now she missed him terribly. Thankfully, she had a packed schedule to fill up her days so she didn't have to think about him every waking hour. Only the ones when she was alone in her apartment.

So she spent as much time as she could in the new BU/MU office. It wasn't hard to do. The remodelers were finished, but the place had to be cleaned and polished, furnished, stocked, and set up for business. There were snags, of course, which she almost welcomed because they gave her purpose and took time to sort out. The wrong couch was delivered. One of the pieces of wall art was damaged in transit. The printer made a mistake on her business cards.

Then there was the fun part—arranging the open house. The invitations alone for the event officially kicking off their new office took her days to hand address, to give the personal touch Summer liked.

Summer came to town the week before the open house and helped, which was not only a relief but gave Bella welcome company. By two days before the party, they were completely organized and mostly handling press interviews and last-minute details with the caterer.

On the Thursday before the big event, Summer left Bella to hold down the fort while she had coffee with a reporter from a business publication who was interested in what BU/MU did. She was using the time alone to set up a filing system on the computer for the counselors, social workers, and lawyers they'd already lined up as consultants. As usual, her favorite radio advice guru, Dr. Sea-Tac, was on in the background as she worked.

Her concentration was broken by what she thought was a familiar voice. She listened more carefully. She was right. Taylor was talking on the radio. She turned up the volume and was horrified. He was talking about her.

"So," Dr. Sea-Tac said in a sympathetic tone belying her harsh words, "from what you've described, 'screwed up' barely begins to cover what you've done with the woman you say you love."

"I already know that part. What I don't know is how I'm going to get her back."

"You sure you shouldn't move on to another relationship? From what you said at the top of the show, you met her after another relationship had ended. Maybe it's time ..."

"No, it's not time. She's the one. You have to help me. Please. I'm desperate."

"I can hear it in your voice. You really mean it, don't you?"

"I absolutely do. I'll do anything. I'm already doing something I never thought I'd do by calling into a radio advice program. I mean it when I say I'll do whatever it takes."

The show host snorted. "I guess you do mean it although I'm not sure I want to have my program described as a desperate last hope. Maybe my listeners have some ideas. Listeners, what do you think? This guy, Teej is his name, got thrown under the bus by his girlfriend because he seriously messed up a work project his lady was managing and kept a very big secret about his former relationship from her. But he wants her back. My lines are open to hear your opinions. We'll hear them as soon as we get back from this commercial break."

Taylor Jordan called into an advice show? If she hadn't heard it with her own ears, she would never have believed it. She wasn't sure if hearing that he loved her on the radio was the most romantic way to find out or the most insulting. She was sure saying those words on the air was something way out of Taylor's comfort zone. *How did he know I'd be listening?* He must have paid attention to what she listened to when he'd been in her office.

Summer returned from her coffee with the reporter as Dr. Sea-Tac came back on the air. Normally, Bella would have turned the radio off as soon as her boss appeared, but she couldn't this time. She wanted to hear what the audience had to say.

And so did Summer as soon as she heard the host explain what the problem was. "Teej? Is Taylor the caller?" Summer asked. "And he's asking for ways to win you back?"

"Apparently. We are about to hear what the audience has to say."

"I'm more interested in what you have to say but I'll shut up until this segment is over."

They both listened as audience members made suggestions ranging from the mundane—flowers and candy—to the over the top and potentially criminal—kidnapping her and taking her up on a hot air balloon ride and keeping her there until she agreed to take him back. Taylor responded to every suggestion, thanked everyone for their help, and pledged to keep working at getting the woman he loved back.

The unanimous opinion of everyone who called in was he deserved to get her back. The callers admired his forthrightness, his honesty, his willingness to take responsibility for his mistakes, and his desperate plea for help.

When the host switched to another caller with a problem, Summer said, "I have to agree with the audience. He sure sounded to me like he meant it."

Some part of Bella agreed. She knew she was weakening, but she mentally shook it off and said, "Maybe. Maybe not. Sounding all honest and forthright now is fine. But if he'd shown how honest he was a few weeks ago, he'd have never found himself calling on strangers to discuss his problems."

Summer didn't argue with her.

But that evening, as she ate dinner alone in her apartment, Bella wished she had recorded the radio broadcast so she could hear his voice again. Especially the part where he said how much he loved her.

• • •

Bella and Summer both got to the BU/MU office hours before the open house was to begin. They fussed with the furniture one more time and rearranged the table with the brochures and fact sheets on their services. Fanned out the paper napkins on the table of treats first one way, then another. The stacks of cups got their close attention as did the playlist on Bella's iPod, which would provide background music.

A birthday cake and plates and forks for the birthday celebration were on a table in the kitchen. A large red ribbon was tacked across the door to what had been the dining room of the house, where the snacks and treats were. Summer had invited a city councilor and a representative of the Neighborhood Business Association to do the honors with the ribbon cutting. The snacks and cake would be served afterward along with a surprise. Summer was being very mysterious about what the surprise was.

As soon as the doors opened at one, people streamed into the building. The living room, with its pale blue upholstered furniture and restful seascapes became so crowded Bella was concerned they were violating fire codes. Many of the consulting counselors and attorneys they would be working with were there, as were curious neighbors, some of the former clients she had been contacting, and a good representation of the business community she'd met through the Chamber of Commerce. Promptly at one thirty, Summer took her new program director by the hand and walked to the red ribbon.

When she had the crowd's attention, she said, "As most of you know, I'm Summer Olsen, the founder of Break Up or Make Up. The woman on my right is Isabella Rodriquez who has been the project manager while we got this enterprise underway and who will now direct the operation here in Seattle. The ribbon we're cutting today officially opens our new office. But before City Councilwoman Jones and George Foster representing the Neighborhood Business Association cut the ribbon, I'd like to recognize someone in the audience. Mrs. Pennington, will you raise your hand, please? We didn't start out on cordial terms, but we've come to understand each other better and to share our concerns about the health of this neighborhood so we welcome your presence here today."

She picked up a pair of scissors and handed them to the two dignitaries. "Now, let's get this puppy open." The duo efficiently cut the ribbon to the cheers of the crowd.

"Before we celebrate another event—the birthday of my new program director—I'd like to make this an official Break Up or Make Up opening by having the first BU/MU letter delivered to someone in the audience today. If you'll please let my messenger get through so he can get the letter to me, we'll conclude the official part of our ceremony."

A young man wearing jeans and the distinctive BU/MU T-shirt appeared as people moved away to let him pass. When he reached Summer, he handed her a legal size envelope. She thanked him, and he disappeared back into the crowd.

"This letter was commissioned by our first official Seattle client and it's for ..." She paused, looked around the room and then, as if surprised, said, "Isabella Rodriquez."

Bella jumped when she heard her name. "For me? From whom?"

Summer grinned at her. "Why don't you open it in the privacy of your new office and find out while I get the cake organized.

When you've read it, we'll cut your cake and sing 'Happy Birthday.'" She turned to the people standing around in front of her and said, "How about a little help getting the cake out to the reception area?"

Curious about what was in the envelope, Bella closed herself off in her new office and opened it. As soon as she saw the first line of the letter, every sense came alive. She knew exactly who had written it.

Dearest Isabella,

I made a mistake. A huge one. I waited to tell you about the mess I'd made with Mrs. Pennington and how I was the guy who vowed revenge on Summer hoping, if you knew me better, you'd understand my actions, at least a little. If you knew I was, at heart, a good guy, then it wouldn't sound so bad when I finally told you what I'd done.

I was wrong. My only explanation of why I thought it would work is I was falling for you so hard and so fast I couldn't think straight. I never knew I could fall in love so quickly. It was outside any plan, any experience, I ever had. So I made the biggest mistake of my life and I hurt you. I'm more sorry than I can ever say.

I miss you. I miss your laugh and your warmth. I miss the way you light up a room, the way you light up my life, the way everything seems better when I'm with you.

I love you, Isabella. You are the most amazing woman I've ever known. If you'll forgive me for being an idiot, if you'll give us a second chance, I'll do whatever it takes for however long it takes to make it up to you.

My Break Up or Make Up counselor said you might be willing to consider my apology if I showed how sincere I was by getting out of my comfort zone to tell you what I'm willing to do to get you back. So, I asked a radio audience for advice (in case you were listening, no, I'm not going to kidnap you for a hot air balloon ride). And I've sent you this letter. If the third time is the charm, maybe what's next will finally convince you. Summer will tell you what it is.

Love,

Taylor

She couldn't stop crying as she read the letter. She knew Summer's fingerprints were all over it, but still she knew how the system worked. The sentence structure may have been Summer's, but the sentiments were Taylor's. He did love her. She was sure of it. And he was sorry. He'd gone so far out of his comfort zone to prove it, he'd hired the very company he swore once to hate.

There was a soft knock, and Summer opened the door.

"So, you ready to meet your letter writer and have him join us for birthday cake?"

"How long have you been plotting with him?"

"He called the day you confronted him in his office, worried about you. We went from there. Do you mind?"

She laughed. "I'd be a poor manager for you if I minded taking on a new client, wouldn't I?"

"Yes, I'd say that was true." Summer perched on the desk and took Bella's hands. "I'm convinced he means every word in the letter."

"Yeah, I am, too." She stood. "So, what's this third shot he talked about?"

"Go out on the front porch and see."

What she found when she got there was Taylor, looking a bit embarrassed, holding a huge bouquet of balloons and drawing the attention of everyone who walked into or past the building.

She stopped outside the front door to appreciate the sight. It was hard not to laugh out loud at the picture of her perfectly serious Viking god looking like all he needed was a monkey and a barrel organ to become a cartoon character. An organ grinder dressed in an expensive-looking suit and silk tie, perhaps, but an organ grinder nonetheless.

"Happy birthday," he said.

"Thank you. And thank you for the letter. It was lovely."

He looked up at the balloon bouquet. "This is for you, too."

"Yes, I can see all the 'happy birthdays' written on the balloons. You look cute holding it."

"If holding a stupid balloon bouquet in public is what it takes to make you give me another chance, I was willing to do it."

She took the remaining steps across the porch to reach him. Circling his waist with her arms, she said, "No one has ever gone this far to try to impress me."

He held her with his unencumbered arm and kissed her hair. "Because no one has ever loved you the way I do." He nudged her forehead with his chin so she would look up at him. "Can you forgive me?"

"How can I not with everything you've done to make up with me?" She rose on her tiptoes and kissed him on the cheek. "Not to mention, I love you. Of course I forgive you."

"You don't know how much I needed to hear you say those words. I love you, too." He looked up at the balloons he was holding. "There's one more thing I need from you."

"What's that?"

"Help. Please. I have no idea what to do with a balloon bouquet. Do you?"

"How about you let them float to the roof of the porch so you can put both your arms around me and kiss me?"

"Now, that I can do." And he did.

"Damn it, Melody," Catherine Bennett said as she slammed into the dolly loaded with banker's boxes her assistant was supposed to be pulling. "You can't stop like that. This thing has no brake lights to warn me." As she steadied the pile of teetering boxes, she followed Melody's gaze to see what had distracted her. She should have known. A man. Dominic Russo, to be precise. And he was definitely a distraction. Mister Dark and Dangerous. Man candy. A professional bachelor with a reputation for notching his bedpost with a new name every few weeks. Name a cliché describing a sexy male, and he fit it. Hell, he owned it.

He also owned one of the most successful public relations firms in Philadelphia and was Catherine's biggest competitor.

"Damn is right," Melody said. "Hot damn."

Catherine bent and rubbed the shin that had borne the brunt of the collision. "You might want to add an 'ouch' in there."

Melody whipped around as quickly as she'd stopped. "Oops. Sorry, Catherine. Are you okay? Didn't mean to hurt you. I was just admiring the scenery." She returned her attention to the man who was now almost at the elevator bank. "Look at those shoulders! And the way he moves. I bet he's a great dancer—and you know what *that* means. He is definitely sex on legs. Wonder who he is?"

"Your encyclopedic knowledge of Philadelphia gossip is failing you. The 'scenery,' as you put it, is Dominic Russo. The Russo Group has offices on the fifteenth floor."

"Of course! Shoulda looked at his face instead of his ass." Melody started toward the elevator again. "If you'd told me my days in our new office building would be brightened by sightings of the sexiest man in the city, I'd have been happier about moving here."

"I'd have used it, believe me, if I'd known it would have stopped you from complaining about all the work it took to move the office."

"You know how much I hate change and loved the old building." Melody looked across the lobby again. "Although the old building never offered us something like that to look at. On the other hand, now that we're in the same building as our competition, we'll always have to be careful what we say when we're …"

The service elevator door began to close, and Catherine interrupted Melody's latest reservations about the new office arrangements to yell, "Hold the elevator!" to her staffer Tom.

But before Tom could hit the "door open" button, Dominic Russo made a graceful move to his left and grabbed the door.

"Thanks," Catherine said as she and Melody pushed the dolly into the elevator.

"Happy to help. Moving's hard enough without having to wait endlessly for elevators." He smiled and the temperature in the lobby spiked. "You're Catherine Bennett, aren't you? I'm Dominic Russo."

"Of course. We've actually met …"

He nodded. "After you spoke at the business roundtable about your firm's approach to socially responsible marketing and business practices. You had so many people trying to talk to you that day, I didn't know if you'd remember me. I enjoyed your presentation. When you get settled, maybe you'd consider repeating it to my staff. I don't imagine I did it justice when I tried to relay the information."

Not remember meeting him? Was he kidding? He was impossible to forget.

If the rumors were to be believed, most of the women in the city would agree. Interesting, because he wasn't handsome in a classic, young god kind of way. His jawline was a bit too strong and his nose a bit too aquiline for the perfect image of the divine. The bits of silver beginning to show in his thick, dark hair and the lines around his eyes and mouth put him out of the age range of most Hollywood hotties.

But all that was unimportant compared to the devastating smile currently aimed at Catherine and the deep, dark, espresso brown eyes that seemed to say he knew everything worth knowing about a woman merely by looking at her. Any woman he turned that look on would have her knees melted in two seconds flat with the rest of her quickly following.

And then there was the body Melody had drooled over. Not to mention the wrapping it came in. Even in Philly's humid summer heat Mister Sex on Legs looked cool and unruffled. The dark suit he wore fit as if he had grown it like skin, not had it tailored. The accompanying white shirt was crisp and unwrinkled, the dark gold and black paisley print tie in a perfect knot, the matching pocket square precisely placed.

Catherine, on the other hand, was both ruffled and wrinkled. Her long hair was mostly pulled back into a messy ponytail; her jeans and T-shirt were rumpled and dusty. There were, she was sure, tracks of perspiration running down her neck and arms from helping to load the dolly with the boxes of client records she didn't trust to the movers. To top it off, she must reek; she hadn't showered yet today.

Naturally, Dominic Russo not only looked good, he smelled good. Like a gingerbread man.

Right. The hot guy smells like Christmas cookies. Nice, Catherine. Not some sensuous fragrance. A kid's holiday treat. You're really out of practice, aren't you?

She would prefer to think she was relying on food imagery because she'd skipped breakfast, but in truth she *was* out of practice. Unless he was a client, staff member, or sub-consultant, she hadn't thought about, dated, or otherwise paid attention to any man, sexy or otherwise, for a long time. With a business to grow and a teenaged son to raise, she didn't have time for a social life. At least, that's what she told her family and friends. What she admitted only to herself was she hadn't recovered from having her ex-husband leave her for another woman. She wasn't about to take the chance of having her ego battered again by a man who would use her for what he wanted then move on to the next female who crossed his path.

Although even at her best, she would have known better than to waste her time thinking about Dominic Russo in any capacity except as someone who did the same thing she did for a living. He was like the statues of perfectly formed men in the art museum. She might like looking at them, but they were blind to women like her, used to lots of attention, and off limits to the masses. He wasn't for amateurs.

Come to think of it, though, he *was* paying attention to her at the moment, waiting for a response to his request. Which was what she should be thinking about instead of mentally concocting some weird thought mixture of art museums, marble statues, and Christmas cookies. If she didn't say something soon, he was going to think she was an idiot.

Finally she got out, "I'd be happy to talk to your staff. But you're right; it'll have to be after we get ourselves settled."

"Not to worry. We'll be here when you're ready." As he let go of the door, he flashed another of his heat-inducing smiles, which Catherine was sure could not only melt knees but also the hooks on a bra. Lord, even her perfectly straight copywriter Tom was blushing from its high wattage. And Melody was speechless, for the first time in all the years Catherine had known her.

Oh, for heaven's sake, she wanted to say to her staff as the elevator began to rise to the tenth floor. *We don't have time for this. We have an office to get set up and clients to attend to.*

Dominic hadn't been in his office more than fifteen minutes when Edie Martin, his creative director, stormed in.

"What were you thinking, Dominic, letting The Bennett Group lease space in our building? Do you really think it's wise to have that group of newbie pretenders eavesdropping in the elevator every day when they're the biggest threat to our business?"

"It's Bennett and Associates, Edie. If you're going to complain about them, at least get the name right. And I'd hardly call them 'newbie pretenders.' They're one of the up and coming PR firms in the city. Everyone in the industry is talking about their approach as cutting edge."

"Why are you letting them in our building where they can spy on us and steal our clients?"

"It's not 'our' building. It's my building." He took the papers she'd been waving around as she spoke. "Catherine Bennett's firm has all the qualifications to be a good tenant, and I've had a hard time filling the space the engineering firm left when it moved. Besides, we already have several other threats to our business, as you describe them, in the building and we've been fine."

"But the other communications firms aren't—*she's* the one— *they're* the people who've been getting too much of the work we should have gotten."

"We have more than enough clients to keep us busy. And we're on track to have the most profitable year in a decade. I'm not worried Bennett and Associates will listen in on our plans through the HVAC system and we'll go under." He could see she was not responding to his attempts to make light of her concerns. "Why don't you think of it another way—now we have all our strongest competitors in one place so *we* can watch *them*."

Edie's face brightened a bit. "Oh, I never thought of it that way. Maybe you're right. Maybe it's a brilliant plan. I hope so, Dominic."

"Now, other than to bitch about Catherine Bennett what brought you to my office this lovely Monday?"

When Edie left, the thought of Catherine Bennett didn't go with her. Dominic's morning encounter with Ms. Bennett had been a welcome start to the day. In spite of being a bit sweaty and in clothes miles away from the stylish suit she'd worn the first time he'd met her, she was stunning. Her olive skin and her dark chocolate brown hair and eyes, which didn't fit with her WASP-y name, had intrigued him from the first. Still did, even though now he knew from a little background research that her coloring was from an Italian heritage as deep as his own. And there wasn't a man alive—well, a straight one—who wouldn't fantasize about the luscious curves even moving-day clothes couldn't hide. She wasn't some stick-thin model who served as a hanger for the latest designer's ideas of fashion. She had the body of a real woman. A real woman with considerable ability and the drive to take her firm all the way to success. It was quite a combination.

Dominic had wanted to get to know Catherine Bennett ever since he'd seen her give her presentation. Mostly he'd wanted to see if she was as smart and interesting one-on-one as she'd sounded on the dais. And he wouldn't mind finding out if she was as sexy in a more intimate situation as she was when she walked across a room in her pencil skirt and stilettos. He was bored to tears with the business dates he'd been stuck with for what seemed like an eternity. Catherine Bennett looked, sounded, and acted different.

And it wouldn't hurt to size up the woman who was making such a splash in his industry. Mixing business and pleasure was what he did on a regular basis. Most of his recent social life, including the women he escorted to the theater or dinner, had been more about marketing his business than about anything personal. At least if he were doing the mixing with Ms. Bennett, he might actually enjoy what he felt he had to do to keep his company on top.

A fixture in public relations and advertising in Philadelphia for more years than Dominic cared to think about, The Russo Group was the biggest, the most highly regarded, most sought after communications firm in the city. Catherine Bennett had only been on the scene for a half dozen or so years, but she'd made a name for herself in a niche he'd never thought about—marketing and advertising for socially responsible companies who wanted to do more than make a profit at any price. He admired someone who could find a new facet to a business he thought he knew cold and owned outright.

He'd told Edie the truth about how he viewed Bennett and Associates—there was plenty of business for both of them. But the fact was, relocating to the building where the big boys played meant Catherine Bennett was moving up in his world. It wouldn't hurt to keep an eye on her.

Or was he making business excuses to do what he wanted to do for personal reasons? And did it matter anyway?

•••

"Ah … Catherine, someone's here to see you." Melody's voice sounded confused or nervous. Something. Certainly not like her usual self.

"I don't have anything on my calendar, do I? Who is it?"

"He's not on your calendar. And he's on his way back now." The call ended abruptly. Very unlike her usually efficient office administrator. And why was she working the phones anyway?

Catherine put down the phone and looked up as Mister Sex on Legs sauntered into her office. That explained it.

"Mister … ah … Dominic. What a nice surprise. What can I do for you?" Catherine tried to be more calm and collected than

Melody had been. All she could really be was grateful she had an important client meeting later in the day and had worn her favorite cobalt blue suit, the one she knew was flattering to both her figure and her coloring. Because to hold her own in the same room with this visitor who always looked like he'd stepped out of *GQ* took the best she had.

Dominic Russo must have a closet the size of Rhode Island. In the two weeks she'd been in the building, she couldn't remember seeing him in the same suit twice. Not that she was keeping track. Okay, yes, she was keeping track. She didn't know why, but she was.

Today's suit was a navy pinstripe number with a white dress shirt and a light blue patterned tie that looked like a William Morris print. A white pocket square peeked out of the pocket over his well-toned pecs. The man knew how to dress. And call attention to his assets.

Oh, for God's sake. Pay attention to something other than his body, Bennett. What is wrong with you, anyway? You don't behave like this.

She forced herself to stop staring at his chest and glanced around the room, hoping her office made a good impression. It looked tidy, at least. Although her artwork hadn't been hung yet, all the furniture was in place: her glass-topped desk and small conference table, the cozy little couch covered in a bright red fabric, the Herman Miller Aeron chair for her, and a visitor's chair next to her desk.

"I wanted to make sure you'd gotten settled," Dominic said. "Although from looking around, I'd say you've done more in the past two weeks than many people manage to do in a month. Your artwork in the reception area is stunning, by the way, especially the image of the woman. I like it. Local artist?"

"Yes, a woman named Jamie Lutz. Thanks for noticing."

"I hope everything about the space was the way you wanted it to be when you moved in."

His interest puzzled her. "Does the building owner hire you to check on all the new tenants this way?"

"You didn't know I'm the building owner?"

She was sure her surprise was visible. "I thought the owner was DR Investments Limited."

He said nothing, seeming to wait for the penny to drop.

Which it did. "Oh, DR. Dominic Russo. Dear God, how could I have been so obtuse."

"You're anything but obtuse. I'm sure there are other tenants who don't know. The management company that handles all the transactions doesn't advertise it, and neither do I."

"But if I'd done my due diligence, I'd have found out. I didn't dig very deep, obviously. When the agent showed me the space and told me the price, I was so excited I didn't do much other than talk to some of your other tenants. All of them, by the way, raved about the building and the management, in case you wondered."

"Good to hear. And I'm happy you're settling in so well." He motioned to the chair next to her desk, which she took to be asking if he could sit.

"Please. Sit. I'm being rude." She returned to her desk chair. "It's been a pretty smooth transition. It's a great building. The location is perfect and the layout very creative. Did you have a hand in designing it?"

"Can't take credit for it, but it is what attracted me to the space. The original developer had gone bankrupt, and it was being sold at a good price when I was looking for new offices. My staff was working in such close quarters, I was beginning to think I'd have to insist they marry each other."

"We were almost there, too, although on a much smaller scale."

"You've come a long way in a short time, haven't you? I've admired your work and how fast you've become such an influence in the business." His killer smile was back, which almost distracted her enough that she missed the compliment he'd paid her.

"It feels like a long time and a short way, but thanks. I'm flattered."

"Not flattery. Just the truth." He rose from the chair and extended his hand. "I won't keep you any longer. I only wanted to make sure everything was as promised. I know you've met the building manager—if you have any problems at all, let him know."

When she took his hand, a pulse of electricity went up her arm, startling her enough she had to swallow a gasp. It warmed her all the way to the base of her neck and down her chest. He clasped her hand with both of his, his eyes holding hers in a look so warm she wanted to turn up the air conditioning. She also wanted to keep the conversation going so she didn't lose the connection with him.

"Uh … yes … the building manager." She swallowed hard. "He's been great. About getting movers in and out, I mean, stuff like that." *Stuff like that?* Where was her skill with words when she really needed it?

Dominic didn't say anything right away, seeming to be as reluctant as she was to break the contact between them. Finally he released her hand. "I'm glad he was helpful." He moved toward the door. "But let me know if you have a problem he can't solve. I'm sure I'll be seeing you around the building." And he was gone.

Catherine sank back into her chair feeling like all the life had left the room, along with most of the air in her lungs.

For more great novels from Peggy Bird, check out these titles:

A Holiday for Love series:

Sparked by Love

Praise for *Sparked by Love:*

"With lies and hidden agendas, you have to wait and see till the very end for all the pieces to fall together!" —Chicks That Read

"A warm, fuzzy romance read. Leo and Shannon are just so sweet together. There is plenty of steam as well. Very enjoyable read for romance lovers." —Wilovebooks, 4 stars

"This book had the Triple 'S' factor for me: short, sweet and sexy . . . a wonderful book." —Red's Hot Reads, 4 stars

"This was my first time reading Peggy Bird. I was pleasantly surprised by not only her writing style, which was very engaging and flowed, but also her characters." —Book Nerd, 4 stars

Unmasking Love

Praise for *Unmasking Love:*

"Spicy and modernized, this story relies on the mystique and romance of Romeo and Juliet, without the bad ending. Peggy Bird brings heat and heart to Halloween." —4 stars, I Am, Indeed

"I love the author's witty writing style, which is present right from the opening lines of this book. Ms. Bird successfully builds deliciously, believable sexual tension between Julie and Trace; you can almost hear the cracks of electricity!"—5 stars, Ellesea Loves Reading

"The story isn't long, but it wasn't rushed. ... Beautifully written and wonderfully engaging."—4 stars, Written Love Reviews

Second Chances series:

Beginning Again

Praise for *Beginning Again*:

"Both Liz and Collins are great characters. Liz is not a bitter middle aged woman, but instead a very strong and brave lady. I really enjoyed *Beginning Again* because it was an easy read that made my gray autumn day a little bit less gray." —Long & Short Reviews

Loving Again

Together Again

Praise for *Together Again*:

"…a very enjoyable romance. I loved the main characters and the great writing. I always admire strong, independent women, so if you also enjoy those qualities in a heroine, and enjoy a well-written romance, I recommend this one." —Night Owl Reviews

Trusting Again

Praise for *Trusting Again*:

"The book moves along at a nice pace and the characters are believable and realistic. It is a well-written story with a wonderful ending!" —Harlequin Junkie

Believing Again

Falling Again

In the mood for more Crimson Romance?
Check out *California Sunrise by Casey Dawes* at
CrimsonRomance.com.